Looking grim, Shiva addressed both Bolan and the SVR agent

"I think we need to talk for a minute. I knew several of those men, or, rather, of them. We've got a problem here."

Suddenly Bolan caught a faint but familiar sound of distant rolling thunder. It pealed on trailing waves down through the gorge. Everyone froze.

The Executioner knew that a battle was raging somewhere to the north. "If you have something you want to say, I suggest we fly and talk. I have a hunch your Major Thornton just found Spetsnaz."

Bolan waited until Shiva boarded the gunship. If the agent didn't come clean about the slaughter they'd found, the soldier was prepared to take matters into his own hands.

Damn the odds. The Executioner would carry on the hunt. As far as Bolan was concerned, he was on his own.

MACK BOLAN ®

The Executioner

DON PENDLETON'S
EXECUTIONER®
THE
TERMINAL OPTION

A GOLD EAGLE BOOK FROM
WORLDWIDE®

TORONTO • NEW YORK • LONDON
AMSTERDAM • PARIS • SYDNEY • HAMBURG
STOCKHOLM • ATHENS • TOKYO • MILAN
MADRID • WARSAW • BUDAPEST • AUCKLAND

First edition December 1997
ISBN 0-373-64228-8

Special thanks and acknowledgment to
Dan Schmidt for his contribution to this work.

TERMINAL OPTION

Printed in U.S.A.

Nothing can excuse a general who takes advantage of the knowledge acquired in the service of his country, to deliver up her frontiers and her towns to foreigners. This is a crime reprobated by every principle of religion, morality and honor.

—Napoleon I
Maxims of War, 1831

There can be no forgiveness for the soldier who betrays his country, who steps all over the Stars and Stripes. There is but one judgment, and I'll be the one who sees that the sentence is carried out.

—Mack Bolan

THE

LEGEND

Nothing less than a war could have fashioned the destiny of the man called Mack Bolan. Bolan earned the Executioner title in the jungle hell of Vietnam.

But this soldier also wore another name—Sergeant Mercy. He was so tagged because of the compassion he showed to wounded comrades-in-arms and Vietnamese civilians.

Mack Bolan's second tour of duty ended prematurely when he was given emergency leave to return home and bury his family, victims of the Mob. Then he declared a one-man war against the Mafia.

He confronted the Families head-on from coast to coast, and soon a hope of victory began to appear. But Bolan had broken society's every rule. That same society started gunning for this elusive warrior—to no avail.

So Bolan was offered amnesty to work within the system against terrorism. This time, as an employee of Uncle Sam, Bolan became Colonel John Phoenix. With a command center at Stony Man Farm in Virginia, he and his new allies—Able Team and Phoenix Force—waged relentless war on a new adversary: the KGB.

But when his one true love, April Rose, died at the hands of the Soviet terror machine, Bolan severed all ties with Establishment authority.

Now, after a lengthy lone-wolf struggle and much soul-searching, the Executioner has agreed to enter an "arm's-length" alliance with his government once more, reserving the right to pursue personal missions in his Everlasting War.

1

"We need to talk," Mack Bolan said in a graveyard voice.

The man from New Delhi took dripping hands off his face, straightened from the sink and glanced in the bathroom mirror of the Washington, D.C., restaurant.

The first hint of sudden violence was the flash of cold killer fury in Sanjay Singh Bahjwani's dark eyes.

The second and life-threatening tip-off was the sleek blade the Indian whipped from his belt buckle. Just like that, the Executioner found himself face-to-face with a human cyclone of pure rage.

Catching the glinting blur of razor-sharp steel in the mirror, Bolan leaped back just as the blade swept past the bridge of his nose. An inch or so closer, and Bolan knew he would have been blinded.

The Executioner could have pulled his silenced Beretta 93-R from the shoulder holster beneath his dark corduroy jacket and drilled Bahjwani in the face, ending the confrontation right there. But he needed the suspected terrorist alive for some hard interrogation.

Bolan surged at his target. Clamping a viselike

grip over his adversary's knife hand, he head-butted Bahjwani's nose. A squelch of bone, blood spraying through the air from a pulped mess that was a heartbeat ago an aquiline centerpiece for a handsome swarthy face, and Bolan had the guy's full attention.

The four-inch blade clattered into the sink under a slick torrent of blood.

But a moment later, Bahjwani proved it was far from over. Somehow the man dredged up raw strength and determination. Even wearing a long black leather trench coat, he proved lightning fast. Snarling through his bloody mask, he slashed a left uppercut off Bolan's jaw, following up with a knee to the soldier's ribs. Any more power behind the spearing blow, and Bolan knew he'd either be sucking wind or reeling from a broken rib.

It was going all the way, Bolan knew, something he had hoped to avoid. Obviously Bahjwani was hellbent on taking the secrets of his dark mission to the grave.

Staggered a step back by another short blow to his jaw, Bolan managed to duck when his adversary launched a looping roundhouse meant to shatter his skull, drive bone shards from his temple into his brain.

As the Indian's fist swept over his head, the Executioner turned it up a notch.

Exploding from the knees, spearing his forearm between Bahjwani's legs, Bolan used his enemy's forward momentum to pick the guy up and hurl him over his shoulder. A moment later, Bahjwani's flight ended. Slamming the floor, the man skidded facefirst toward a guy in a suit who had just crept out of one of the stalls. No sooner had he appeared than the newcomer retreated into his stall.

Pumped on adrenaline and cold anger, Bolan rolled for Bahjwani. The Executioner was reaching for his Beretta 93-R when the Indian bellowed and leaped to his feet. Once more he showed Bolan he wasn't about to go quietly. So be it.

The Executioner held his ground for a heartbeat as Bahjwani charged him. A quick shuffle to the side, then Bolan hammered his hands on his opponent's shoulders. Two forward steps, and Bolan hurled the guy through the air.

A human missile, Bahjwani blasted into the bathroom mirror. Shattered glass, tainted with running crimson, rained over the man as he crumpled over his black travel bag.

The Executioner unhooked one of four sets of plastic handcuffs from his belt, looking up as the guy from the stall crept past him. A groan from the Sikh told Bolan it was finished, at least for the moment. Quickly Bolan wrenched Bahjwani's hands behind his back and clamped the cuffs on his wrists.

Crouched over his adversary, Bolan turned his head and found a big guy standing near the bathroom door. There was a look of indecision on the guy's face, his eyes torn between anger and fear. Bolan also read the look of authority on the guy's face.

"You mind telling me what the hell is going on here?"

"You the manager?" Bolan asked.

"That's right."

Bolan produced his Justice Department ID. "I hope you didn't call the police."

A face-to-face with the local law would slow him down. Given what Hal Brognola had dug up from the Stony Man computer network about Bahjwani the past two days, the Executioner knew he had to keep moving quickly, unimpeded by a litany of questions and formalities with the police.

"Not yet."

Bolan nodded. The manager had a look about him that told the Executioner the guy would deal with it. Good. These days, when the slightest hint of trouble showed, too many people either called a lawyer or a cop, or went shrieking all over the talk-show circuit to air their dirty laundry. Bolan felt a small sense of relief, gratitude toward the manager. With maybe a few minutes to spare, he could be gone from the restaurant, ready to bombard his prisoner with a barrage of questions.

The Executioner had earlier seen the wad of cash Bahjwani had pulled out in the parking lot to pay the cabbie. Digging the U.S. dollars out of the man's pocket, Bolan gave the thick stack a hard look. There had to be somewhere close to ten thousand in the stack, all Franklins. The soldier peeled off five C-notes and placed them on the sink.

"That should cover the damage."

"Plenty enough to even keep me quiet. I'll give you three minutes to clear my restaurant."

"I appreciate that."

The manager took the money, then disappeared.

"What about my money?" Bahjwani growled.

Bolan pocketed the wad. "Charitable contribution."

"To what?"

"The families of three FBI agents some of your pals gunned down two days ago."

Bahjwani snorted. "A thief, as well as a man of violence."

"Welcome to America."

Bolan took a long moment to stare down into the Indian's hate-burning gaze. Quickly the soldier gave a mental assessment of recent events regarding activity by suspected Sikh terrorists in the Washington area.

For Bolan, it had started at Dulles International Airport when the Indian stepped off his flight from New Delhi, two hours earlier. From there, Bolan had followed Bahjwani's cab to this restaurant across from Tyson's Corner. It had been a start for the Executioner, but for three FBI agents who had raided an apartment in Greenbelt, Maryland, two days earlier, it had ended in sudden death. There, two suspected terrorist associates of Bahjwani had been cornered by the FBI. The two men from New Delhi had gone down fighting, taking with them three good lawmen in the firefight. The FBI had found assault rifles, plastic explosives, even a LAW rocket launcher in the Greenbelt apartment. None of the Indians had been left alive to provide any clues to their intent. Bolan intended to find out why suspected Sikh terrorists were moving into the Washington area. And if there was any doubt the soldier had his man and was onto a trail of some murderous mission, it was long gone once Bahjwani lashed out like some cornered animal.

"Just who are you?" Bahjwani rasped, spraying flecks of blood.

"For you, I'm the end of the line unless you answer some questions."

"I am but a mere businessman from India. This is an outrage! I have all necessary paperwork to be in your country."

"Oh, I can be sure it's necessary, all right. What business are you in, Bahjwani? Cutlery?"

After picking up the Indian's travel bag to examine later, Bolan hauled the man to his feet. "You made a call from Dulles, I assume to let your friends know you're in town. After we have a little talk outside, we can go see your buddies."

Defiance hardened Bahjwani's bruised features. He gave a strange laugh. "Very well. I will play your game."

"If you consider your impending death a game, I can arrange that."

"The only death I am interested in is the total destruction of anything and anyone who is not Sikh."

"Sounds to me like you want to cooperate."

A cold smile cracked the Indian's shattered mouth. He nodded several times. "I see one man who snuck up behind me and got lucky. We shall see how your luck holds."

The Indian was going to play it hard, to the bitter end. Just like that, Bahjwani had changed his song and dance. What Bolan now read in the man's eyes was cold arrogance. All right, so Bahjwani thought he was leading him to certain death, Bolan thought, march him right to his terrorist comrades, into the guns.

A graveyard smile danced over the Executioner's lips. "If my luck doesn't hold up, you'll be the last one to know."

BEFORE THEY ENTERED Vienna, Virginia, Bolan got the street and the address of the town house out of Bahjwani. It then became obvious to the soldier he wasn't going to get much more out of the man except attitude and lip.

Bahjwani sat stiffly in the passenger seat of Bolan's rental sedan. The Indian's face was swollen, lopsided, but anger and arrogance still flamed in his eyes. He spit blood off his lips, then crooked a grin at Bolan.

"Why do you not just kill me, end it? Or do you not have the stomach for cold-blooded killing?"

With traffic starting to thin against the full on-slaught of night, Bolan kept the rental cruising smoothly into the heart of the suburban town. There were still too many cars, too many people either driving or walking. Factor in the strings of shops and restaurants, minimalls and clusters of homes and split-level town houses rising from side and back streets...well, if the hit turned hard, it would be all Bolan could do to keep innocents out of the line of fire. Unless, of course, he kept the action confined to the terrorist safehouse. Either way, Bolan was going in, fast and furious, braced for anything but hoping to bag another prisoner or two. As for enemy numbers he would be facing, Bahjwani had already declined to give him any answer other than "Enough."

Bolan looked at Bahjwani. "And disappoint your friends? No, I've got plans for you. A bullet through the head is too damn easy for a guy who tried to slash my eyes out."

Bahjwani chuckled. "Your time will come. Soon. You see, that is the problem with you Americans. You have become soft, weak from wealth and animal pleasures. You live in a narrow world where only money and creature comforts and pleasures of the flesh matter. You do not understand, nor do you care how your rape of the world's resources and your exploitation of the poor of the earth has made you devils in human skin. You and your ilk are held in either righteous hatred or utter contempt by any and all beyond your borders. It is all coming back—how do you say in your country?—in your face."

"The only thing I know is that two of your pals killed three FBI agents a couple of days ago. Skip the philosophy, the only thing *in your face* is life and death—your own."

"Precisely. It is what we are all about."

Finally Bolan started to believe he might get somewhere closer to the truth, and decided to work Bahjwani's philosophy angle.

"Killing Americans, is that what you're all about?"

"It is merely a step in the right direction. We, as Sikhs, are a minority in India. We are outnumbered by the Hindus, who make up roughly eighty percent of Indians and own and control the wealth in my country. We have been pushed around, put down and held in either tolerance or contempt by Hindus and Muslims for too long. We are virtual slaves in a system that still rewards those who have too much, while it tramples those who have too little. We are, I believe you would say, much like your American blacks."

"You would say that—I wouldn't. Right is right, wrong is still wrong in any corner of the world. Any way you want to rationalize it, what your pals did was murder."

Bahjwani's stare turned cold. If it wasn't for the cuffs pinning his hands behind his back, Bolan knew the guy would have gone for his throat. For damn sure, the Executioner was sitting on a viper, but one with no fangs at the moment.

"If you're so indigent," Bolan said, "how is it you can jet all over the world, buy up real estate from a people you hate and walk around with enough American dollars to choke a sacred cow?"

Bahjwani smiled coldly. "We have a concerned third party. That is all I wish to say."

Bolan let it ride. Someone was sponsoring the Sikh terrorist group from the shadows. But who? Why? Answers would come in time, the soldier determined, one way or another.

Bahjwani indicated a turn, and Bolan took it. Slowly he rolled down a long street lined with split-level town houses. With a bitter prewinter chill in the air, the street and sidewalks were deserted. The street ended in a cul-de-sac. Bahjwani pointed out the safehouse. There, Bolan found a light on behind the curtain of the first-floor bay window.

The Executioner parked, curbside, three houses down from the safehouse. Killing the engine, he surveyed the street for long moments. It was a quiet residential neighborhood, the suburbanites unaware a den of potential killers had moved in among them.

Bolan pinned Bahjwani with steely eyes. "You understand what will happen to you if something goes wrong?"

The Indian smiled. "Completely."

Briefly Bolan reflected on Bahjwani's perceived Sikh oppression, if for nothing else than to measure the kind of enemy he was up against. It was the same age-old argument: a person had what someone else wanted, and if that someone had to, he or she would take it by force. Essentially that same line of thinking had always landed every thief, murderer and rapist behind bars, or in the grave.

Recalling what the team at Stony Man Farm had dug up, Bolan knew the Sikhs were indeed a minority in India. The dead terrorists in Greenbelt had also borne the name Singh on their passports, their flights also having originated in Delhi. Sikh, originating from the ancient Sanskrit word *shishya*, translated into "disciple." Not only were some Sikhs religious fanatics, their religion a rough adaptation of the mysticism that shrouded Hinduism, with its belief in reincarnations, spells, curses and worship of countless gods, but they were also fierce warriors and had proved themselves competent and loyal soldiers in the Indian army. Most Sikhs took the surname Singh, which meant "lion."

To some degree, it was also true that the Sikhs had often been brutalized and abused by their rival and hated Hindu brothers. More than ten years ago, the Indian army had even attacked the Sikh's sacred Golden Temple in Amritsar, killing hundreds of Sikhs in a vicious raid, followed by a murderous siege of the temple that lasted for several days. What the Sikhs essentially wanted was their own independent state within the borders of the Indian subcontinent, autonomous turf much like Bangladesh or Sri Lanka.

Still, the bottom line of Bahjwani's game was terrorism, murder and mayhem—land, money, power and control. It was the same dark hunger that had driven men throughout human history to commit countless atrocities, more often than not against innocents who wanted nothing more than to be left in peace.

Bolan reached over the seat and fisted an Ingram submachine with attached sound suppressor. Opening his door to a blast of icy air, he hauled Bahjwani out his side.

"Nice and easy, stay in front of me," Bolan said, marching the Sikh toward the safehouse.

Bolan gave the safehouse and surrounding homes a hard look, finding it strange there was only one light on in the house and no vehicles in front of it. Something felt wrong. The enemy had to be lying in wait.

Only way to do it, Bolan knew—through the front door, and take them down as they came.

As they moved up the sidewalk, Bolan asked, "Is there a code, a knock that signals them it's you?" When Bahjwani hesitated, looking defiant, the soldier added, "I'm standing you right in front of the door. If they decide to start blasting away, it's your head."

"Two knocks. Stop. Three knocks. Stop. One knock."

Bolan checked the rear, moving up the short flight of steps. The quiet darkness shrouding this neighborhood was about to be shattered.

Topping the steps, the Executioner pushed Bahjwani forward, placing the man directly in front of the door. Bolan rapped on the door with the series of knocks. No answer. He waited for several stretched seconds, listening, but there was no sound of movement on the other side of the door.

Combat senses on full alert, the Executioner tried the doorknob. The door opened with a soft click, light from the hallway beyond spilling over Bahjwani. Grasping the man by the back of his coat, Bolan burst through the door. The hallway was empty. Moving Bahjwani along, he checked the stairs leading to the upper level. No sound, no indication of movement from anywhere in the house. Ahead, at the end of the hallway, the soldier saw part of a living room and nothing more than a sofa and two chairs.

Instinctively Bolan checked the base of the wall and the ceiling for trip wires.

A second later, the Executioner discovered his gut instinct paid off, but it was too late.

The infrared laser beam was almost invisible to the naked eye at first glance. But Bolan spotted the pencil-thin light just after Bahjwani crossed through it. Snapping his head sideways, Bolan found the light knifing from a small black box set in the middle of the kitchen floor. The box was giving off a low beep, a red light on top of the transmitter flashing.

Ingram low by his side, warning bells going off in his head, Bolan pushed Bahjwani toward an open area beyond the kitchen.

The Executioner spotted the C-4 bomb in the middle of the living room, with a radio receiver and what looked like a time-delay detonator planted atop the pile of plastique. At the first and only glance he gave the plastic explosive, Bolan knew there was anywhere from fifty to one hundred pounds, more than enough to bring down the whole house.

Bolan jerked Bahjwani along, racing down the hall in lockstep, expecting the C-4 to blow. With Bahjwani cuffed and unable to run at full speed, every passing heartbeat throbbing in the soldier's ears.

Barreling out the door, Bolan launched himself off the stairs. Out of the corner of his eye, he glimpsed Bahjwani also taking flight. No sooner did Bolan hammer to the lawn, roll, than he was surging for a BMW parked next to the safehouse.

The Executioner was airborne over the vehicle when the night was shattered by a roaring, apocalyptic ball of fire. Behind him, Bahjwani was bounding over the vehicle just as a brilliant mountain of fire vaporized the town house. Shock waves ripped the air and shook the ground beneath Bolan with hellish seismic force. Jagged walls of debris rained over the cul-de-sac, or sailed down the street behind dragon tongues of fire. Wreckage pelted Bolan's cover, crushing the BMW's roof. As the soldier hugged the ground, riding out the blast, he saw Bahjwani make a sudden flight for freedom. Before Bolan could blink, the Indian tucked his legs and flipped over on his back in a smooth lightning move, melting into himself, it seemed, to get his cuffed hands in front.

The man bolted.

Then the night came alive with an assault from the rear.

Braving the shower of fiery debris, Bolan hit a combat crouch. He was swinging up the Ingram when he spotted a sleek vehicle surging from the far end of the street. Autofire was stuttering from a passenger window, an assault rifle jumping around in the hands of a dark silhouette.

The first target was Bahjwani. Obviously the Sikh terrorists had already decided not to leave even their own alive, if captured.

The hail of bullets kicked the man off his feet as if he'd been bowled down by a wrecking ball.

Then the tracking stream of autofire swept for Bolan, but the Executioner was already on the run. Chased to cover behind another parked vehicle, he came up firing, holding down the Ingram's trigger. He caught sight of a small object bounce under the frame of his sedan before the enemy vehicle stopped, then squealed in reverse down the street. The Executioner's first and only return fire raked the windshield of the enemy vehicle. He saw shadows duck as glass blew over them, then they were gone in a final peal of smoking rubber.

Knowing what was next, Bolan flung himself beside a Honda Accord as the grenade erupted. The blast lifted the sedan several feet into the air and sheared off the driver's door, hurling glass and metal fragments across the street.

Rising from cover, the Executioner took in the hellzone. Shadows were spilling into doorways down the street, but no one ventured outside. So far, he heard no distant sirens, but that would quickly change.

A moment later, the Executioner stood over Bahjwani. There was no need for him to check for a pulse, as the man's intestines were leaking all over the street, his unseeing eyes staring skyward.

It was clear to the soldier the Sikh terrorists would commit suicide, even kill their own to carry out their mission.

Right then, that was enough for Bolan.

But somehow he would get the answers he needed.

The night was still young.

2

It would be his second and final trip to America. The first time he had arrived in Washington, D.C., via their cell in New York City, six months earlier, Mokhan Singh Adjan had quickly discovered many things about this land and its people that he had long suspected. First, and most striking, was the obscene wealth of the country. Second, and just as appalling, was the apparent ingratitude of its people for all they had. Indeed, for all this country had in material richness, still so many either seemed to take their privileges for granted or thrashed around in envy and rage, wanting more, wanting what the other man had. Strange. Even the shabbiest of apartment buildings were gleaming diamonds compared to the hovels of his village in the Punjab. From New York through his stay in Baltimore and finally setting up the mission in Washington, he found that even the poorest of Americans could afford nice clothes, shoes and a car, and could feed themselves at any time of the day. Coming from a land where his countrymen bathed in crocodile-infested rivers and streams, he was amazed to find there was running water, clean and pure, in every building, public or private, where anyone could drink or bathe himself. Here, a man even had the privacy of his own toilet, didn't have to suffer the indignity of squatting over a hole in the middle of the village in full view of everyone.

Here, there was food, drink, luxury and pleasures of all manner he had never dreamed of knowing in India. What, he wondered, would a typical American do if he or she was suddenly thrust among the infinite sea of the desperate, poor and starving in his homeland? Would there be compassion? Would the privileges provided by America still be taken for granted? Would the whining about perceived discrimination and injustice be stopped? Would he or she quash senseless animal desires to take what others had?

This was a land of madness. In many ways, Adjan couldn't wait to send his message to this land of bloated ego and material lust, then be gone from this barbarian country.

As he sat in the eastbound traffic jam on Interstate 66, Adjan wasn't quite sure, though, how he really felt about America in the final analysis. Torn between envy and resentment, admiration of these filthy rich Americans and his own desire for wealth and privilege, he refocused on what had to be done. Adjan warned himself his perception of America and its people, perhaps distorted by the sting of his own poverty, could not be allowed to shroud his vision with blind rage. A cold, steely determination was the only mind-set called for. The mission was critical for the future of all Sikhs in the Punjab, after all. Victory here meant receiving the other half of the payment from their sponsors back home. Failure…well, certainly neither he nor Bant Singh Maraka would allow himself to be captured by the American authorities.

When it was done, when they had made their statement to America, they would flee the country, disappear into the Himalayas of northern India. The sponsors had gone through too much trouble, too much expense for them to fail now, from the phony passports, to all the paperwork laid out for the string of safehouses from New York to Washington, to the rental and used vehicles, bought off the seedy car lots with the seemingly never-ending flow of cold American cash available to the strange but deadly coalition of their sponsors. Finally, there were the contacts on American soil who had provided them with the necessary firepower and escape route. Yes, Americans helping to kill Americans. Indeed, a land of insanity.

Never mind there was a problem last night when Bahjwani had arrived at their Vienna safehouse. They had already factored in the risks, such as treachery by their American cell, raids by the FBI or Justice Department. It was why they needed a vast number of safehouses, contingency plans. No sooner had Adjan seen Bahjwani exit a vehicle with the tall armed figure last night than he and Maraka had activated the time-delayed plastique. Then they'd slipped out the back door, reaching their rental car, which they had parked down the block. Of course, they had to make certain the job was done. Bahjwani couldn't be left alive, but their brother Sikh had already known the deal going in. Even though they had silenced Bahjwani forever, his captor had apparently escaped their hail of bullets. But it didn't matter. They had changed vehicles and hunkered down in another Virginia safehouse to ride out the night. The following morning, they were up early and out the door, listening to the traffic reports on the radio of their used Jeep Cherokee.

Now they were inching along in the far right lane. Long, agonizing minutes ago they had cleared the Vienna exit, slithered at a snail's pace into the endless sea of nose-to-nose metal. The sky was overcast, a gunmetal gray, with reports of snow. Somewhere near the off ramp to the Beltway an accident had the eastbound traffic locked to a standstill. Perfect.

It would be like shooting rats in a barrel.

Adjan took his eyes off a man in a brand-new Mercedes, one car ahead, and looked to Maraka's driver's side. He decided the man in the Mercedes would be his first victim.

Maraka gripped the steering wheel tight, his bearded face carved with tension. "Why are Americans so angry? Everywhere we have gone, we have seen the same mindless rage. They talk only about money, they seek only to dirty one another with their animal passions."

"It is because they have no soul," Adjan said, watching the man in the Mercedes pound his steering wheel and mouth curses. "They want to believe that because they have material richness, they have everything, that they are better than the rest of the world. But from what we have seen, they have nothing I want. Their love of money only makes them more insane, they have reduced their women to either she-men or whores who will bed with any manner of man. Their children they have either abandoned out of selfishness, or the brood of their vile seed turn against their own blood."

"Then they need to know a day in the life of the truly poor."

Adjan looked at Maraka. "No. They need to know death. They need to be made aware their lives are no more important than the poorest farmer in the Punjab. Our sponsors were right. This is a land of no honor, no pride. Only madness. It is time to do it."

Quickly they stuffed their belts with a half-dozen banana-shaped clips for their AK-47s. The Sikhs snugged tight the belt holding pouches of Soviet F-1 fragmentation grenades, then both of them slipped a coiled rope with a grappling iron over their shoulders. Adjan gave the concrete sound barrier ahead a hard look. He figured it was a twelve-foot climb over the wall. From there they'd run into the woods, leave their weapons behind but hold on to their M-63 machine pistols. Somewhere near Route 50, it shouldn't be too difficult to find a suitable carjacking victim. Since nearly all traffic was attempting to surge east for the city, a quick but low-key retreat west was the only logical way.

Adjan sucked in a deep breath and chambered the first 7.62 mm round. "Now."

They burst out their doors, both knowing that the first few moments were absolutely critical. The idea was to claim as many victims as they could while making their way for the sound wall.

Holding down the assault rifle's trigger, Adjan

blasted a long, blazing lead finger into the front passenger window of the Mercedes, watching the man's head explode in a pink mist. Without hesitation, he sprayed another vehicle, found the Honda Accord packed with four men in suits, their eyes bulging in terror, their mouths wide to vent screams of horror.

The foursome tried to duck the tidal wave of glass pounding over them, but they never managed to even hug the floor or beg for mercy. Adjan stuck the barrel of his AK-47 through the glass shards, chopping them into bloody sieves at point-blank range. Before he emptied the 30-round clip, the vehicle was a metallic coffin of twitching limbs, awash with dripping crimson curtains.

Just as Adjan had anticipated, pandemonium erupted. Behind him, screams tore the air. Horns started to blare in panic, and figures disgorged from the four lines of jammed vehicles. But Maraka, he found, was also hard at work. Startled or terrified faces became death masks as Maraka raked a merciless stream of blazing lead over men and women running pell-mell over the highway. Adjan saw one man attempt to play hero. He was a big, muscular hulk in white denim coveralls. The hero bounded over the hood of his pickup truck, nearly reaching Maraka, but Adjan cut him down with a 3-round burst.

Holding their ground, the Sikhs turned up the heat of murder.

If the motorists ducked in their vehicles, Adjan and Maraka rolled right up to those cars and scythed them where they cowered. If they ran trembling onto the highway in shock and horror, the Indians riddled them with lightning messages of sudden death. Race, gender or age, it didn't matter to the terrorists. If it moved, it was fair game.

Within moments, any space around the bumper-to-bumper traffic was littered with bodies, beds of glass and free-flowing streams of crimson. With the concrete barrier separating the east- and westbound lanes, vehicles and their occupants became paralyzed prey for the Sikh slaughter.

Firing indiscriminately on the move, the Sikhs made their retreat toward the sound barrier, expending one clip after another.

As countless screaming and cursing commuters scrambled for the westbound lanes, Adjan and Maraka then began to lob armed grenades in all directions. Two, maybe three more male commuters attempted to play hero. But the Sikhs were pumped on adrenaline, had seized the initiative and were hell-bent on flight. Any man who charged their blindside was cut down by volleys of autofire, crucified into vehicles or kicked to the highway.

Detonating grenades added more chaos and horror to the highway of death. Fireballs blossomed to the rear of the Sikhs. With each lethal egg holding sixty grams of TNT, capable of spewing out razor steel fragments in a twenty-yard radius, mangled bodies took to the air, riding the tongues of roaring fire clear across the westbound lanes. One victim slammed through the windshield of a vehicle on the westbound flow. A screech of rubber, and that sleek luxury car was whiplashing all over the highway. A truck bearing the logo of a cable-TV company clipped the rear of the Lexus and flipped on its side, showering sparks to a thunderous rending of metal. Behind the truck, in a chain reaction of smoking rubber and sliding vehicles, cars became missiles, twirling like crushed children's toys over the barrier. A wall of smoke and fire now sheeted nearly a quarter mile of traffic to the west. Gas tanks erupted, hurling passengers and vehicles in all directions.

Adjan and Maraka each tossed two more grenades into the frenzied mob stampeding its way over the barrier or heading for deeper cover west in the traffic jam. The two men flung the grappling hooks, catching the lip of the sound barrier.

Adjan couldn't resist hosing down two more commuters with one final burst of his assault rifle. To the din of crackling flames, screams of agony and horrific rending of metal impacting on metal, the terrorist scaled the wall.

As MACK BOLAN swung his Saturn rental car onto the grounds of the Annandale apartment complex, he felt as if he carried the outrage of a nation in his gut, the grief of all Americans on his shoulders. That morning fifty-plus innocents, on their way to work, had been butchered by two men of vague description while they sat in the I-66 traffic jam. The slaughter had been swift and indiscriminate, and obviously well planned. In addition to the dead, countless more had been injured, many of them critically, with the body count expected to rise.

The identities of the killers were no mystery to

Bolan. He had missed his chance to take them out the previous night, and now those men were responsible for the slaughter on I-66. Worse, the terrorists seemed to have vanished off the face of the earth. The Executioner strongly suspected the butchers had help getting into, then out of the country.

Bolan needed hard intel if he was to pick up the hunt.

Hal Brognola had done some furious digging through various contacts in the intelligence community during the day, called in some markers to get Bolan what he needed to pick up the scent of the terrorists. Supposedly the man with all the answers was holed up, alone, in this apartment in Virginia, a mere few miles from where the Sikhs had slaughtered their helpless prey. Brognola had hinted at the man's identity, but no one seemed to really know exactly who he was. All the Executioner knew was the man was former CIA. More specifically, according to the big Fed, it was rumored he was part of an elite shadow group that had worked for years with and for the Company under the guise of national security, a group whose identities and borderline illegal or outright illegal activities had been kept secret from even the President. Perhaps the man with the answers was looking to come back into the fold. Or did he have his own agenda? Bolan wondered.

It didn't matter. The former CIA operative was the only lead the soldier had at the moment.

Bolan killed the engine, then looked down the lot, instincts flared up for trouble. He saw a black four-door Plymouth swing into the mouth of the complex and realized they had been on his tail all the way down Route 50. The thought fleeted through Bolan's mind he was being set up. The one intelligence source that had led him via Brognola to the man with the answers had been found executed in his condo on Wisconsin Avenue three hours earlier.

The Plymouth slowly turned down an adjacent stretch of lot, vanishing. Bolan was marked—he was sure of it. But by whom? Why?

The Executioner unzipped his black leather bomber jacket, giving himself quick and easy access to the shoulder-holstered .44 Magnum Desert Eagle, and cautiously he stepped out of the Saturn. Combat senses on full alert, finding nothing but twin lines of dark and vacant vehicles up and down the lot, he ventured into the building.

The door to the hallway grated on rusty hinges, and Bolan made a mental note to keep his ears tuned to just that sound. Moments later, he came to the unit Brognola had identified. He was about to knock when a gravelly voice that seemed to call from the bottom of a tomb said, "It's open."

Bolan hesitated, then reached for the knob, his hand sliding toward the hand cannon.

As if the man knew what his visitor was doing, he said, "No need for all that. We're alone, and I have no firepower."

Bolan checked the empty hallway, the ceiling. If there were any cameras monitoring the hall, they were well hidden. Slowly he opened the door and stepped into the apartment. He found the man, sitting in a leather recliner, near the drawn curtain to the

patio. The stench of cigarette smoke was a thin veil
covering the stronger smell of slow, rotting death.
Bolan had seen this type of man before, the assassin
who had experienced the worst the human race had
to offer, but never quite this way. Maybe it was the
fact that there was nothing in the apartment except
two nightstands, the man, his chair and another recliner facing him. Maybe it was the soft yellow light
that struck the side of the man's skeletal face. Maybe
it was his swept-back shock of white shoulder-length
hair, revealing bluish purple scars and indentations
across a high, heavily lined forehead, the scars tell-
tale evidence of near misses from the business end
of an adversary's bullets. Whatever it was, Bolan
sensed the presence of death in the room, but it was
an undetermined threat.

"I had a feeling they would send someone like
you," the man said.

Bolan's gaze narrowed, the soldier getting the distinct and slightly unsettling feeling in his belly that
this man knew, or believed he knew, something
about him. For several moments, he stared at the
skeletal figure, his gaze taking in the contact, the
eerie, bare surroundings.

The man was dressed in a black sports shirt and
gray slacks. Barefoot, he sat with one leg comfort-
ably crossed over the other. He lifted a cigarette to
razor-thin lips. On the nightstand was an ashtray
overflowing with butts, a half-empty bottle of Wild
Turkey, a shot glass, what looked like a floppy disk
and a bottle of Zippo lighter fluid. True, the man
wasn't armed, not with any visible firepower. But

there was a sheathed *wakizashi* at his feet. The short sword was notorious for its use when defeat or dishonor loomed over the Japanese samurai, who would then commit seppuku by disemboweling himself.

"Close the door, friend, and take a seat."

Bolan did just that.

"Left it unlocked. I would have done the same. No need to worry about watching your back, friend. That door in the hall squeaks loud enough to wake the dead. That cannon you've got under your coat probably has enough stopping power to take out two men with one shot, if you get them lined up, front to back."

Bolan watched as the man filled his shot glass, then killed it in one gulp. If he was intoxicated, it didn't show. In fact, the man's ice blue eyes seemed to shine with a crystal-clear penetration into the Executioner's soul. As Bolan sat, he observed the man's skin was so white it almost seemed to glow. Again it could have been the effect of the only light in the unit.

The man refilled his shot glass, then torched a cigarette with his lighter. "I was expecting a call from the contact who gave your man my location. Since I haven't heard from him, I am assuming the one who led you to me has been, uh, terminated?"

"Apparently, as you might say, with extreme prejudice."

"They still use rather primitive methods to extract information. Do you know if it was quick?"

"I understand he took one right between the eyes. That's about as quick as it gets."

"So, my former employers are running scared. And so it would seem you know something about my involvement with— Well, I'll refer to them as 'those people.' No matter, those people can come through the front door, start blasting away with their silenced little pistols if they wish. It was bound to happen. They tend to delude themselves with a self-serving image of themselves as the good guys. One thing I can be sure is I won't see the sun rise." The man gave Bolan an odd smile. "And since you're talking to me, since I'm sure you were followed, I would suggest you watch your back when you leave here. If you are who I want to think you are, then what I'm about to reveal to you may tell you all, or it may tell you nothing."

"Just who is it you think I am?"

The man smiled cryptically. "I'm not in the mood for any bullshit, son. I've been around for a long, long time. I can be sure you know the kind of things I've seen and done while those people wrapped me up in the Stars and Stripes. Just for starters, I was in Vietnam for ten very ugly years. I heard the tales of this one soldier who went home to bury his family who was killed by the Mafia. Seems this soldier went on to virtually wipe out the Mafia. Then, suddenly, he just disappeared."

A knowing smile cracked the man's razor lips. Bolan felt his gut knot with tension. Over the years, during the endless miles of his hellfire trail, he had been forced to claim new identities, even undergo plastic surgery. A warrior could die, or be thought dead, but his legend would always live on. If the guy thought he knew something about those years, then Bolan would let him believe what he would.

"I'm not here to trade war stories," the Executioner said.

"That right? Then tell me, how do you like sitting with a dead man?"

"For a man living on stolen time, you don't look all that concerned to me."

The former operative flashed an easy smile, sipped his whiskey. "Not in the least. They gave me less than three months to live. Cancer. You can say I really don't give much of a damn about anything, much less myself anymore. I stay floating on enough booze and pills to keep me from going down to the nearest fast-food restaurant with an M-16 and a handful of grenades and taking about thirty or forty poor schmucks with me. I can tell you, withering up into a pile of bones from cancer is no way for a warrior to die."

Bolan glanced at the short sword. "If you plan on sticking yourself, do it after I leave. I don't have the time to hear your life story. I need background on the slaughter this morning. I was told you had some information."

The man chuckled and sipped his drink again. "What I have, friend, is far better than mere information." He tapped his skull, pointed at his eye. "I have knowledge. Care for a drink?"

"No, thanks. I'm listening."

"I've had so many names over the years, so many handles, that even I've forgotten my real name.

Whatever it was, well, it isn't important. Let's just call me...Smith. For the sake of politeness.''

Courtesy was the last thing on Bolan's mind. "What is it you know?"

"I know that we live in dishonorable times, friend. I know that the world doesn't run on love—it revolves on the almighty dollar, which equals power and control. With a few serious bucks in your pocket and the bank, the ugliest man in the world will look good to any woman. I can see you growing impatient. If I was Japanese, I'd say you were being most discourteous, even disrespectful.''

"We're not Japanese. Your point, or I'm gone."

"The point is this, friend. The human race is on the verge of total annihilation. In fact, your government, the same government I heaped enough sins on my head for to put me in hell for all eternity, is seeking to accelerate Armageddon.''

"I think you'd better back off the bottle and the pills. I want some straight answers, not end-of-the-world babble.''

Smith put steel into his voice. "The real power structure of this country is not in the executive mansion or in the hallowed halls of the Capitol. Every day, the world's population, especially the populations of the Third World countries, is growing at a rate that can eclipse in a single year the sum total of every human being that has ever walked this planet. Natural resources are shrinking, to the point that in a few years the only source of energy the world will have will be nuclear. Food will become so rare that to eat a handful of rice will be more cherished than all the gold in the Federal Reserve, and it could well happen by the turn of this century. But that's only a start.

"There is a clandestine power structure within the ranks of those people, and they have plans to initiate the apocalypse, to bring about their vision of a Utopia following the holocaust. They can do it through nuclear proliferation, or they can unleash a virus that they have genetically mutated from the Ebola virus, a strain, it's rumored, ten times more potent. They can and will use this strain to selectively wipe out whole continents, what I have heard them call 'the lesser peoples' or the 'subhumans,' who can't feed themselves, who are a blight and a drain on the world. What I'm telling you is that what happened yesterday was only the tip of the iceberg, a mere beginning by this group who will use whatever cannon fodder is at their disposal. The Sikhs just happen to be their first guinea pigs.

"Now, both of us know that the only thing holding it all together is a few good men. But our numbers are being depleted every day. I'll tell you why. You see, the truly hypocritical aspect of man is that he talks about peace on earth, about goodwill to his fellow human beings, but man doesn't want peace. It's neither in his nature nor his own interest to have peace. War is evolution. War reduces the threat of man being overrun by himself in a population explosion. War contains three of the four horsemen. It can bolster, elevate man to new heights—it reconstructs entire economies, whole civilizations. All you have to do is look at the Germans and the Japanese to understand my theory that war is evolution. They came out of the rubble to become the world's leading economic warriors. 'Welcome to the new age, kiss my ass,' is what they're saying.''

"So, you're telling me there is a group within the United States government that wants to unleash World War III? According to you, acting on their own.''

"You catch on fast. Forget all the talk about a New World Order coming out of the White House. The real thing is hard at work, run by a group that calls itself the Council, right under the noses of those in this nation who want to think they're in charge. Mind you, this isn't some conspiracy that reaches into the Oval Office, but it's close enough.''

"If this is true, if they even believe you know so much, how come they've let you live this long?''

"Oh, I'm not in hiding. Fact is, the best place to hide from your enemies is to hunker down right under their noses.''

"And, of course, you have hard proof of this conspiracy.''

Again the strange death's-head smile. Smith picked up the floppy disk and held it like a trophy. "This, friend, makes me the most dangerous man in the world.'' He dropped the disk, popped a pill and washed it down straight from the bottle. "Over the years, myself and a few close associates have accessed eyes-only documents. It took some time, but what we decoded were so many documents...that disk is, well, call it leverage. They take it, maybe there's a few copies laying around in inaccessible places with my associates.

"What's on that disk is just about everything your government doesn't want you to know. If the public at large caught wind of what's on that disk, I can assure you there would be revolution in the streets, the masses would storm the White House. There would be an anarchy that would end democracy in the United States as we know it. I've got all the hard, cold, chilling facts. Names, dates, events, the whole sordid cover-up of so many strange happenings, so many illegal activities by Big Brother...well, you can understand why they would want me dead. Everything from the Roswell incident in New Mexico to details of past administrations sanctioning assassinations of well-known heads-of-state.

"I know for a fact that the narcotics epidemic that has the Western World locked in a death grip was an intentional creation of those people. I was there in South America during the seventies. It doesn't take a genius to figure it out. We've got satellites orbiting the earth that can pinpoint a Boy Scout camp fire in the woods of, say, the state of Washington, and they can't find cocaine-producing laboratories in the lower Americas?"

"Corruption," Bolan said, putting an edge in his voice. "I've heard something about it. Look, you're starting to sound like one of those right-wing militia groups that wants to overthrow the government because they think everyone who isn't like them has given them a tough time of it."

Smith chuckled. "Maybe, but they don't know

what I know, nor do they have the pair between their legs that I've proved countless times that I've got hanging. They don't know that the Company helped to create the narcotics industry, the same conspiracy within the conspiracy that helped get those Sikh terrorists into and out of the country.''

"The ones responsible for what happened on I-66 yesterday are gone, is that what you know?''

"Of course they're long gone. Back to India. Never to be seen again.''

"How do you know that?''

"Same way I know the cocaine epidemic was created to give Third World countries a viable product with which to compete in the world economy. The idea, friend, is salvation by any means of evolution it takes. This same group I'm telling you about, who helped expand the worldwide narcotics black market, was also responsible for forming a paramilitary organization which, several years ago, was going to seize the oil fields in the Middle East—once again all cloaked in the Stars and Stripes because, hey, Uncle Sam represents all that's good and righteous. How do I know we were going to take the oil fields away from the Arabs? I was in charge of the operation. When it was set to get off the ground, well, some top brass got cold feet. Right after the operation was aborted, the ones who didn't flee to some remote hellhole in the world suddenly started dying off.''

"I'll ask you one time. Who's financing the Sikh terrorists?''

Smith's expression melted into a grim mask. "Why, the Russians, of course, specifically the

GRU...and that circle I mentioned within the Company."

"The Russians and the CIA are holding hands to promote world terrorism?"

"Why should that surprise you? Ever since the Berlin Wall came down and the rest of the free world chose to lie to itself about how beautiful it was that the Russians were going democratic, well, there were just too many damn hard-nosed old party-liners who read the writing on the wall, who were essentially out of a job. The SVR and the GRU, traditionally at each other's throats, are now making strange bedfellows. When the cold war ended, that also took away the monster villain for our intelligence community to fight against. What I'm saying is that there are those on both sides who want to restore the old order. But this time, they'll link up to create something that encompasses the elements of both sides, sort of a pooling of talent. That's the Council and their vision of the New World Order I've been telling you about. Have you heard of Ivan the Terrible? And I don't mean the Middle Ages Russian czar who murdered his son in a fit of rage."

Bolan said nothing. He was taking everything in, but with healthy skepticism. Still, if this former black-ops agent was on the level, not deluded by booze, dope and paranoia, then the Executioner knew he would leave there latched on to a trail of conspirators as potentially deadly as any he had ever encountered.

"Obviously you haven't, but unless you're close to the core of the intelligence world, you wouldn't have heard of the man anyway. His real name is Ivan Slobovka, he's a major in the GRU, headed an elite Spetsnaz unit that has terrorized everyone from the Afghans to the Israelis. He disappeared when Russia started thrashing around in her attempt to be like us. Word is, he's resurfaced.''

''India.''

''More specifically in the Punjab region, the home of the Sikhs. He's set up his Spetsnaz shop near the Himalayas, and he's recruiting.''

''And he's linked up with this inner faction of those people?''

Smith smiled coldly. ''Like I said, watch your back, don't trust anyone you may become involved with. They're selling death, they're marketing anarchy—that much is obvious. Exactly where they intend to strike next, however, what their prime objective is... Well, maybe you can find out.''

''You've got a long way around of getting to the point.''

''Not really. It all connects. It's the same people who have been around for more than two decades. You're going to be dancing with shadows, soldier, so you might as well know some background in order to understand what and who it is you're fighting.''

''Why the Sikhs?''

''Because Ivan essentially failed with the Palestinians. They came to realize that a bunch of Arabs killing in the name of God didn't work. All it led to was fanaticism. Now they've got people who want something—their own independence. Figure a man who will kill for himself is a whole lot cleaner than a man lying to himself about killing in the name of God.''

Suddenly Bolan heard the hallway door groan open. Right away he came alive, unleathering the Desert Eagle.

''If nothing else, I've at least made believers out of those people,'' Smith said, smiling toward the apartment door. ''I'll tell you this, friend, they aren't the good guys.''

Out of the corner of his eye, Bolan saw Smith douse the disk with lighter fluid. On his feet, the soldier glimpsed the shadows fall over the crack at the bottom of the apartment door. Silence.

The clack of a lighter, then a pungent stench like burning rubber knifed into the Executioner's senses as Smith torched the disk.

Bolan was already moving for the deep shadows of the living room when the gunners came through the door. There were two of them, armed with Glocks with sound suppressors. They were sweeping the room, coming in, one high, one low.

Chugging sounds split the dark as they sprayed the apartment. The intruders managed to squeeze off several coughing rounds before Bolan went to work.

From a combat crouch, he stroked the hand cannon's trigger, all but decapitating the high man with a thundering .44 blast. No sooner did shock register on the low man's face as he tracked on for the dark shadow that was Bolan, than the soldier drilled two hollowpoints through the invader's chest. Twin explosions of blood and shredded cloth followed the two corpses into the hall.

Pivoting toward Smith, knowing he had to get out of there in a hurry, Bolan found the white-haired ghoul on his knees. Before he could say or do anything, the Executioner saw that the man had gutted himself with the short sword. But it was the strange, almost peaceful smile on Smith's lips that startled Bolan for a stretched second. With his blood streaming and guts oozing to the bare floor, as he wrenched the sword sideways and up, the former agent toppled. An ominous kind of serenity became the man's death mask.

There was no time to linger. His mind buzzing with a slew of bad questions and some grim leads, Bolan went through the balcony door.

A war was brewing in the Indian Himalayas. If Smith was right, then the Executioner knew he would be going in alone, unable to trust even his own side.

It wouldn't be the first time, Bolan knew, when the enemy was faceless, might come roaring at him from the shadows.

The Executioner set his mind, all fire and steel, for an all-out rampage.

3

Ivan Slobovka despised his handle of "Ivan the Terrible." Of course, if any man called him Ivan the Terrible or Ivan the Dread to his face or even within earshot, the Russian would shoot him in the head, on the spot. That was the single greatest plus he could think of, being compared to the Middle Ages czar who slew countless Russians at the slightest whim or suspicion of treachery. Slobovka knew his reputation preceded him, the calm before the storm, to produce a chilling fear in his comrades in both the GRU and the SVR.

He couldn't help but smile as he thought about how much blood he had shed to earn the infamous handle. From the early days of the Czechoslovakia invasion to the Afghanistan debacle, the sum total of nearly thirty years of killing both the enemy and executing his own over any displays of treachery or shirking of duty had stapled him as the most ruthless and dangerous man since Stalin. Fear made men obey. It was that simple.

Major Slobovka of the GRU, Russian Military Intelligence, only hoped the fear he produced in the hearts of his Spetsnaz commandos and his Sikh allies carried them through this day of assassination.

Too much was at stake to suffer any setbacks now. Indeed, a revolution was poised to sweep his Motherland. By his design, the Kremlin would eventually be stormed and torn down by force, then rebuilt in the image of a new communism. It was already happening, in the form of the initial groundwork, at least.

Only yesterday, the Sikh survivors of the American mission had returned to New Delhi. Recruited and groomed under the iron tutelage of his Spetsnaz shock force, they were merely the first in a small army he wished to create and export to unstable countries bordering the former USSR. Those Sikhs were now in hiding in the Punjab, hailed as conquering heroes, returning to the worship and glory of their fellow Sikhs. Slobovka had warned the Sikhs to keep a low profile. He didn't need unnecessary attention.

Right then, Slobovka had his gun sights set on far bigger and more important game than unarmed American civilians.

Of medium height and build, the major would have easily melted into the congestion of Old Delhi, the walled fortress city of temples, mosques and bazaars that had once known the glory days and the iron hand of the British Empire. But the pale flesh of his stark, chiseled face with its sloping forehead and high cheekbones made him stand out, a foreign viper, even as he tried to appear inconspicuous in the mouth of the alley on Nataji Subhash Marg.

Everywhere dark-skinned Indians teemed in the madness of the Chitli bazaar. They hawked everything from fruit and vegetables to worthless jewelry and trinkets, or secretly sold rare and valuable tiger bones or skin bought or stolen from the poachers who threatened to render the Asian tiger extinct on the subcontinent. There were rickshaws and cabs, cows, camels and naked urchins, lurching pell-mell in all directions. It wasn't unusual to find an elephant lumbering through the streets, or spot a king cobra slithering, unmolested, revered as it was as some sort of god by the Indians, through an alleyway.

Women in tunics, saris and sarongs balanced wicker baskets on their heads as easily as he might brandish the M-63 machine pistol tucked in its shoulder holster beneath his dark windbreaker. The weight of the machine pistol and the half-dozen F-1 grenades in webbing beneath his coat reassured him he wouldn't be bothered by the countless beggars, pickpockets and potential muggers of all ages. This was a country chosen by himself as a staging point, more out of necessity, with its proximity to Pakistan and Afghanistan, than out of desire. It was the beggars he loathed more than anything about the country. They swarmed in any city of India, he knew, and he thought of their lives as nothing more than he would give consideration to stepping on a cockroach.

The beggars were no problem. It was a handful of the CIA *kalorshniks,* criminals, lurking all over India that Major Slobovka had to be wary of. Not to mention, of course, his own people, some of whom had been ordered by high-ranking officials in the legitimate SVR to terminate him, annihilate his Spetsnaz force, uncover the operation he had in mind.

He had one advantage at the moment, but even his

own natural paranoia made him doubt his conviction that he could trust the agents of this special department. After the attempt of his country to go democratic, the old guard of the former KGB had created a new and secret department. Many former KGB agents and more than a few GRU officers who had nothing to do but monitor the treachery of Russia's countless satellite states, had flooded into this new secret Department X. The SVR—the former KGB—and the GRU had pledged to put aside personal differences, form a union that would restore order to the Motherland. Democracy, Slobovka had witnessed, didn't work when a country had to be fed. The plagues of the West—drugs, crime and unemployment—had descended on the masses who had once worked for and relied upon the state to provide for their needs. Alcohol abuse and suicide had reached staggering, epidemic proportions. If something wasn't done and quickly to turn the tide of the evils of democracy, Slobovka feared Russia would descend into an anarchy that could see an internal nuclear conflict erupt.

The alliance of the old guard of the former KGB and the GRU was made even more strange by defecting CIA agents who had their own agenda for creating a New World Order. Some of those agents Slobovka had met personally, and they had assured him cooperation in his plans to export global terrorism. Those particular CIA traitors were interested in money and personal gain, but Slobovka had his sights set on something more noble—the salvation of Mother Russia. In the long run, how the New Order would be established was still in its genesis, and would be determined by the Council. In the short run, though, terrorism would be used to unleash anarchy in targeted countries.

While whole governments were selectively wiped out, Slobovka and the CIA traitors hoped to step in, using small armies of malcontents—such as the Sikhs—allied with their own secret commando battallions to seize the reins of power. It was, indeed, very risky, marching into volatile regions of the Middle East, various states within the Soviet Union that believed they were independent of Russia. But Major Slobovka, hunted as he was by even his own countrymen, believed there was no other way than to attempt one final march to glory.

Unfortunately there were traitors among the ranks of Department X, sleepers now in place in Delhi. And Department X was created exclusively to handle sabotage and assassination. The worst, the deadliest of Russia's assassins, Slobovka knew, worked for Department X. To have an assassin from Department X coming for him was the worst-case scenario. Every man had to come under close scrutiny; every shadow had to be watched. Assassins from Department X were the equal of the Japanese ninja—silent, stalking superkillers.

Slobovka came alive when the hand-held radio beneath his coat beeped. Taking the radio, surveying the crushing madness of the street for any sign of danger, the Russian spoke into the hand-held.

"Yes."

"They have just left," Captain Mikhail Petrov stated.

"Get your teams in position. I am on the way. You know what to do, comrade."

"Yes."

When Petrov ended the communication, Slobovka swiftly headed up the alley. The American ambassador to India and his diplomatic envoy were en route, the convoy of limousines having just passed through the gates of the Chandragupta Diplomatic Enclave. Relying on intelligence gleaned from his plant among the American diplomatic contingent, Slobovka put the time frame together. Perhaps twenty minutes as the convoy made its way east, across the city, finally rolling north up Mahatma Gandhi Road. But the entourage would never reach its destination. The Americans were set to meet with Guru Singh Soorboka, revered leader of the Sikhs. Soorboka didn't want a Russian presence in the Punjab, and knew about the secret base in the Himalayas. The guru feared the Punjab would become another Afghanistan battlefront for the Russians.

Word had reached Slobovka that Soorboka was going to lead the Americans straight to Adjan and Maraka, via his own clan of informants. If they were captured, the major had no doubt the two Sikhs would betray the location of both the clandestine GRU base and the training camp where the major's Spetsnaz forces were entrenched with their Sikh cannon fodder.

On the move, Slobovka brushed or shouldered his way past urchins and beggars, ignoring their shrill voices pleading for money. The ambush couldn't fail. Of course, Soorboka would hear of the trap, attempt to flee into hiding in the city. With GRU eyes and ears all over Delhi, it would be no problem tracking down the guru and executing him. Given the previous day's events in America, there was now outrage voiced by the West toward the Indians. But that provided the double-edged sword Slobovka wielded. There was now strong anti-American sentiment among the Indians, as the United States rattled its saber, demanding justice for those who were slaughtered on Interstate 66. It certainly helped, Slobovka knew, that he could move, unimpeded by the Indian authorities. The endless supply of funds, pilfered from the Russian Mafia, helped finance his operation, both in India and his Motherland. Bribery was the most necessary of tools. Every man in any land loved money.

At the wide, tree-lined avenue of Mahatma Gandhi Road, Slobovka searched the congestion of humanity. All around him, he saw a sea of bikes and rickshaws, cabs and cows, domed mosques and temples. Everything seemed to swirl in the midday haze. More vendors, more crushing humanity. An eerie screeching raked the air. Alarmed, the major whirled, discovering several rhesus monkeys leashed to their master. Cursing, Slobovka searched the avenue for his people. Stone buildings and grimy bungalows pocked the avenue like a leper's sores.

Under the glaring eye of the sun, the Hindu legions were bathing in the muddy slush of the Yamuna River, even though the air was cut by a chilly wind, now that the monsoon season had ended. Noise, dust and the stench of raw sewage assailed Slobovka's senses. North, he heard the rumble of thunder and spotted the lumbering steam train as it bridged the river. For a few moments, the major fixed a hard eye on the walls of the Red Fort. Inside the fort, the Sikh delegation was waiting to betray his efforts. Slobovka only wished he had the time, and the manpower, to storm the fort and slaughter the Sikh traitors. But there was too much open space inside the fort, which was now guarded by Indian soldiers. A head-to-head confrontation with the Indian army wouldn't only bog him down, but it would also anger the corrupt officials who were taking his money to conceal his efforts in their country. At least in the cluster of humanity in the streets of the city, they stood a good chance of vanishing into the teeming throngs, slipping out of Delhi. Of course, a team of his most trusted Spetsnaz commandos would be left behind to hunt down the guru.

South, Slobovka spotted his team. The Sikhs had been ordered not to wear the wine-colored turbans or their shorts or carry the sword of their long-standing military tradition. Instead, they were garbed in nondescript, loose-fitting tunics that concealed AK-47s. Waiting inside parked vehicles, his own Spetsnaz troops would unleash their RPGs when the convoy showed.

Slobovka kept to the other side of the avenue, moving toward the Raj Ghat, where Mahatma Ghandhi had been cremated after his assassination in 1948. Now the Raj Ghat was nothing more than a spacious park stretching down the muddy banks of the Yamuna.

The major had been told by his informant that the convoy wouldn't be escorted by the Indian authorities, that five limousines would proceed up the avenue as if they were nothing more than part of the traffic cluster.

It was exactly how Slobovka found them, several minutes later.

Five limousines, with dark-tinted windows, nose-to-nose, rolled with the snail's pace flow of cabs, cars and cows.

Slobovka palmed an F-1. From his position, he moved in on the rear of the miniconvoy while Petrov and six other Spetsnaz commandos and an equal number of Sikhs converged on the limos from the north. The major already knew the windows were bulletproof, the doors armor-plated. The only way to make certain the ambush succeeded was to blow the limousines to countless pieces. Whoever attempted to escape from the initial wave of explosions would be cut down by automatic-weapons fire.

Slobovka and his shock troops went to work with grim and deadly precision.

The major lobbed his steel egg beneath the chassis of the fifth limo. Before the hellbomb blew, lifting the vehicle off the ground, warheads from RPG rocket launchers were slamming into the hoods and doors of the targeted vehicles. Screaming and utter chaos erupted, and a stampede of people and animals fought to clear the killzone as fireballs rocked the air with rolling thunder.

Slobovka glimpsed bits and pieces of ragged flesh taking to the air as he closed on the ring of fireballs. Unflinching, he surged on, hurling two more grenades into the firestorm. Doors opened on the two intact limos. Armed figures disgorged from the vehicles, but Slobovka joined his shock force in a scissoring cross fire of automatic weapons.

M-63 machine pistol flaming in his fist, Slobovka mowed down two big Americans in dark suits and sunglasses. They toppled beneath spraying clouds of blood, their Uzi submachine guns jerking for a long moment in dying spasms.

Jagged sheets of metal hammered the street. An icy coldness descended over the major as he stepped toward the crackling flames and twisted wreckage. Something bloody and torn was crawling from a drifting wall of black smoke. Slobovka discovered the wounded man was his American informant, Peter Stivens.

His face streaked with blood, Stivens looked up at Slobovka. "You told me...you would wait until they were inside the fort.... It wasn't supposed to be this way...."

Slobovka grinned at the traitor. "Welcome to my New World Order, comrade."

As they stampeded and screamed from all directions around him, Slobovka held his ground and emptied the rest of the M-63's clip into the traitor's face.

4

"Before we land at Safdarjang Airport, maybe we should spend a couple of minutes getting to know each other, Colonel Pollock."

The Executioner was seated directly across from the man he knew only as Shiva. Aboard a military jet, the flight arranged by Brognola in mutual agreement with the CIA, the soldier figured they were due to land in New Delhi anytime. Except for the pilot, copilot and the man who had taken an obvious handle for the Indian mission, Bolan was alone. Two duffel bags, one for each man, held weapons and clothing that would be necessary for a recon or hard probe into the icy wilderness of the Indian Himalayas. All paperwork had been prearranged, with Brognola contacting the appropriate Indian officials, to allow Bolan and his CIA teammate free and armed movement through India. They would even bypass a customs inspection. Once clear of the airport, the Executioner would be armed with his .44 Magnum Desert Eagle and Beretta 93-R, but leave the Uzi submachine in his travel bag. He would have to wait to see what the Company operative had chosen as personal firepower. At the moment, Bolan wasn't certain he could trust the man, but he was stuck with Shiva.

It also remained to be seen if the agent was a destroyer of worlds like the Indian god whose name he'd borrowed. For damn sure, the Executioner would be going into India with the full deadly intent of shattering someone's world.

For hours, as the jet streaked into the darkness, the Executioner had pored over the intelligence gathered from Stony Man Farm on Ivan the Terrible. From what the file read on Major Ivan Slobovka, Bolan knew he was faced with a formidable foe. Slobovka had been the spearhead for countless Spetsnaz forays that spanned nearly three decades and three continents. From the invasion of the Czechs, to Afghanistan, to destabilizing a half-dozen small African nations, to attempts to arm and finance terrorism in the Middle East, aimed specifically at Israel, the man had made a bloody climb up the ranks of Soviet Military Intelligence. According to Stony Man intel, Slobovka's specialty in Afghanistan had been the wholesale and indiscriminate slaughter of captured mujahideen, not to mention that the GRU major had wiped out entire villages in the Russian-Afghan conflict, innocents he suspected of harboring or arming the fierce mountain guerrillas. Ivan the Terrible was even known for personally executing his own men if he even suspected they were less than loyal.

But several years ago, the major seemed to have just vanished. There were reports, gleaned from CIA counterintelligence, that believed Slobovka had spent those years forming a small army of Spetsnaz commandos for reasons unknown. It appeared that Ivan the Terrible had resurfaced in the Himalayas of northern India. And Bolan knew the major was the one responsible for exporting terrorism to American soil. But why? What was the Russian's main objective? It all smacked of some sinister conspiracy. And the strange, paranoid words of the black-ops agent who had gutted himself haunted the soldier.

Bolan put down the file and peered at Shiva for a long moment. The Company special operative was a tall, broad-shouldered and imposing figure with green eyes and the same sort of ghost white skin, drawn razor-sharp over chiseled features, Bolan had seen on Smith. Shiva, like Smith, was also a chain-smoker, likewise inclined to work on some hard liquor. But there was something straightforward in the man's demeanor; his eyes were not as penetrating and full of paranoia as Smith's had been. Unfortunately neither Brognola nor the computer wizards at Stony Man Farm could come up with anything that would back up the strange story Bolan had gotten from Smith, other than a few loose ends that the man was in all probability precisely who he had told Bolan he was—a black operative who had seen plenty, and most likely knew too much.

Beyond Smith, all Brognola knew was that the CIA had been scrambling around India, even before the Sikh attack on I-66. Apparently the Company knew far more about the terrorist operation than it was letting on. But what, exactly, did the CIA know? What was it hiding? At the risk of stepping all over "friendly" toes, Brognola had gone straight to the President in order to have "Colonel Pollock" attached to the team that would hunt down the terrorists.

Shiva sipped from a fresh glass of bourbon. "You haven't spoken since we left Andrews, Colonel. I get the feeling you don't particularly like working with a Company operative. Something's telling me you'd rather go it alone."

"My duty is far more important than what I want or don't want."

"I see. Well, we both have our orders, I assume, even if we don't like those orders. I'm not looking to step on official toes, flex muscle or dance around about who's in charge. But I get the strong impression we need to get a few things straight. My orders are we're together but each one of us is, I was told, in charge of himself. I want to tell you up-front, I intend to work with you, not against you. We've been sanctioned by both our own government and the Indian government to do whatever it takes to hunt down the bastards who murdered innocent Americans who were doing nothing more than trying to get to work. We're both after the same thing."

"I can't be sure what it is you're after. But I'm looking for answers."

"To what?"

"When I find out, I'll let you know something."

Shiva started to frown, but the expression never quite took hold of his granite features. "All right, Colonel, I'll spare us both the pep talk, stick to cold facts. The Indian government is outraged that they've got an explosive terrorist situation on their hands, and they want it resolved quickly by any means necessary. Satellite recon has proved there is air traffic, to and from Russia, into India, flying regularly over Afghanistan, down through Pakistan. You've seen the photos. Russian Antonov transports have been pinpointed at a remote site in northwestern India near the Pakistan border. We even believe they've flown in the component parts and put together at least four, maybe five Mil Mi-24 attack helicopters. Whatever's happening, it smacks of another Afghanistan.

"That the Sikhs have been identified as the assailants responsible for the butchery on American turf doesn't surprise me, nor does it surprise me the Russians would use them for whatever the hell it is they have in mind. The Sikhs have a long-standing and fierce military tradition in the British army. This wouldn't be the first time in India that there has been a Sikh uprising. What they want, their own independent state called Khalistan, is a clearly defined objective for them, but it's one the Indian government will never allow. It was two Sikhs who assassinated Indira Gandhi in 1984, if you'll recall, but there were also Sikhs killing Sikhs when their sacred Golden Temple came under attack by the Indian army. There have been other assassinations, but much less heralded or notorious, by the Sikhs in their country. We're dealing with a militant minority of determined, tough warriors, many of whom were trained by the Indian military and served in the army.

"Now, in light of what happened this morning to our own ambassador and his diplomatic entourage, we have carte blanche to bring to justice those who are responsible. Only I get the impression bringing any terrorist back to the States to stand trial isn't on your agenda.''

"I'll let them make that call.''

"And we both know what that call will most likely be.''

"If it comes down to us or them, you think you would act any differently than what I intend?''

"I want justice, Colonel, not vengeance.''

"I never get the two confused. As for my orders, I have none other than cooperation with the CIA, up to a point.''

"If you're looking to be so cooperative, how come I get the feeling part of your job is to watch me?''

"Maybe that's only your perception.''

"Or a guilty conscience, is that what you really meant to say?''

"Maybe we've said enough already. I think we should just wait and see how it all plays out,'' Bolan replied.

"Maybe. Maybe if you let me in on what it is you think you know, because you sure as hell act like you do know something, I can provide some input that might make how it all plays out a little smoother.''

Bolan was silent for several moments. He debated how to proceed with the CIA agent, given what he had learned about the inner circle of conspirators in the Company who may or may not be working together with renegade elements of a joint SVR-GRU operation. Finally Bolan decided to let the man in on what he had learned, his encounter with Smith, if for nothing else than to measure Shiva some more. Bolan didn't leave out a single detail, covering everything from the allegations of Company-sponsored conspiracies to engineer the world market of narcotics traffic, to the operation meant to seize the oil fields in the Middle East, right down to the sudden hit on Smith's apartment and the man's suicide.

When Bolan was finished, Shiva took a deep swallow of bourbon. The man looked unsettled.

"I know the man you spoke with. I worked with him first in Southeast Asia during the Vietnam War, then in South America during the late seventies. I'll spare you the history but I can tell you he was a stand-up act, not some raving paranoid all boozed up looking to fly off the handle with a chip on his shoulder. What he told you was pretty much the truth. There's a rumor about an inner but renegade faction of ex–CIA operatives, I repeat, 'ex-black operatives,' who have some agenda with the Russians. We've suspected this for some time. Unfortunately what we don't know about this coalition is a lot. We're pretty much going in cold."

"You have a plan, I assume."

"I've got leads. Whether they're solid, we'll know soon enough."

"I was briefed we'll be linking up with a joint CIA-Special Forces strike force in the northern Punjab."

"One thing at a time, Colonel. The first thing we need to do is rendezvous with a contact we've been able to establish, a sleeper in place in Old Delhi. Seems the sleeper's sitting on the Sikh guru who was to meet with the American ambassador this morning before they were blown clear across the Yamuna River. I had two men among that diplomatic entourage who were supposed to offer the guru safe haven in exchange for what he knew."

Bolan narrowed his eyes.

Shiva looked irritated. "What is it, Colonel?"

"You pretty much glossed over my encounter with your pal. It strikes me as a little strange you have very little to add to his story."

"What's to tell? What he knew, we already know. He was terminated by this renegade faction. You got them first before they got you. End of story. I can't add much more, except that the man was playing a losing game. National security comes first. The man had become far more than a liability—he was a menace."

"Meaning the truth would have hurt somebody. Meaning this faction may not be so renegade after all."

Shiva's jaw worked a little, and anger flashed through his eyes. "If they're getting official support, then I intend to uncover the who, what, where and why. But whatever support this renegade group may be getting is not coming from my people. My experience in black operations has taught me one very simple fact. All any renegade operation needs is what I call the three *c*'s—cash, connections and capability."

"From what I've been able to gather, it would appear that the GRU major we're looking for has plenty of all three. It would also appear, at least on the surface, he's been getting some help from our side.''

"Look, Colonel, what is it you want from me?"

"The truth."

"The truth is there's corruption in every institution of government. Whoever plays that game for their own gain is eventually rooted out and dealt with in no uncertain terms."

"I get this real bad gut feeling I can't even trust the people who are supposed to be on our side. But that's just a fact of life."

"So, deal with it."

"Oh, believe me, I intend to."

"I'm not sure I care for what I think you may be implying, Colonel. I can assure you, I'm about the only one on this operation you'll encounter who may be as clean as the Himalayan snow."

The Executioner said nothing. Actions, he knew, always tightened up any loose ends, always revealed the true nature of a man's heart.

"Shall we call a truce, Colonel? Agree to work together on this?"

"I'll take you at your word on what you said about being as pure as the driven snow."

"Good enough. Once we land, we're going to need each other, more than you want to believe at the moment. You've been briefed. We're going up against Spetsnaz." Shiva paused, then added, "One detail I neglected to mention. Our contact in Delhi is SVR."

The Executioner's gaze narrowed, and he felt a time bomb ticking in his gut. And he was prepared to explode at any second at the first hint of betrayal. If the Company agent was lying to him, or leading him into a trap, then Shiva would find his world shattered first on the Executioner's hit parade.

IT WAS TIME TO MAKE an example. By chance, the perfect opportunity had arisen to make the necessary demonstration.

Major Slobovka was clenching his jaw, suppressing the volatile rage he always experienced before he taught a man the ultimate lesson. At the moment, he was listening to the concerns, no, the whining of Adjan and Maraka. The Sikhs wanted concrete details about how the Russians intended to land the Sikhs their own state of Khalistan, and they wanted to know when they could receive the rest of their money. The men were concerned the Punjab was about to come under attack by the Indian army after the assassination of the American ambassador and his diplomatic entourage that morning. The Sikhs sounded to Slobovka as if they were losing their nerve.

Slobovka had other, more important matters to deal with than Sikh malcontents. First he was poring over the grid layout of this region in northern India. Surrounded by a dozen of his Spetsnaz commandos, the major was hunched over the large wooden table while Captain Petrov monitored the radio, awaiting word from their recon force that had gone out to investigate an area near the Jhelum River, where sudden enemy activity had been reported. Slobovka chewed on his mounting fury, listened to the howling wind batter the canvas of the large tent.

Outside, a snowstorm had smothered the gorge of their compound at the base of the Himalayas along the Pakistan border. Covered in snow, everything was white, adding still more camouflage to the nets draped over the bulk of their two Antonov transports and the five Hind attack helicopters. The problem was Slobovka might have to move higher up the Himalayas, erect a temporary base on a suitable glacier. The worst-case scenario was pulling up stakes altogether. If that happened, he would move the operation to a secondary base he had previously erected in the remote wilderness of Tajikistan, the second-lowest southern frontier of Russia along the Afghan border next to Turkmenistan. The weather, though, was now a major concern. The Himalayas acted, he knew, as a natural barrier to any severe snowstorm that could blanket the plains stretching away from the impenetrable mountain range. However, nature had chosen to act in a sudden, angry and inexplicable manner. Snow had been reported to reach as far south as the edge of the Thar Desert. Bizarre.

Slobovka had never been one to believe in God, much less some force of divine intervention, but a nagging feeling in the pit of his belly was making him wonder if some supernatural act was at work to hinder his movement, his plans. Had nature conspired against him, forced him into a state of near paralysis so that his enemies could move in while he was pinned down by the storm?

The major straightened, pinning Maraka then Adjan with a fierce look. Both Sikhs stood near the closed flap of the tent, their heads wrapped in the traditional turban, their wiry frames swathed in long wool coats. The defiance in their dark eyes didn't escape Slobovka. If anything, he begrudged the two some respect. They were outnumbered and surrounded by his commandos, all of them toting AK-47s. As a fighting unit, Slobovka knew Spetsnaz men were some of the toughest, bravest soldiers in the world. All of his people were combat-hardened shock troops who would only accept death as the last resort, as the only evidence of defeat. Yet the Sikhs acted as though they could handle themselves against his commandos, use nothing more than their curved swords to lop off their heads, stand tall and unflinching as if bullets couldn't kill them.

"We have problems at the moment, my Sikh comrades. The weather is proving a hindrance to our mobility. We believe a strike force, either Indian or American, has located our position and is now en route. We must prepare for an attack. This leads me to the conclusion that for some time there has been a traitor or traitors in the Punjab."

"You indicated Guru Singh Soorboka has fled into hiding in Delhi," Adjan said. "Perhaps he contacted this strike force and led them to our position."

"Perhaps, but I have discovered he was not working alone. As for Soorboka, I have my men hunting for him as we speak. They will succeed in silencing his tongue for good, or they will die where they stand."

Adjan stiffened. "We have pledged our complete

loyalty to you in return for certain guarantees. We intend to honor our commitment. You are not suggesting, I hope, that we are responsible for this sudden turn of events?''

''Not at all. And indeed, you have shown your loyalty and valor regarding our joint mission. As you will continue to do. I need every available man, including my own Spetsnaz troops and you and every Sikh we have armed and taken under our employ, if an encounter with an unknown enemy is mounting around us. As for what you did in America, it was only the beginning.''

''But the beginning of what?'' Maraka demanded. ''I am beginning to wonder if you even know what it is precisely you intend to accomplish. We have not even received full compensation for the success of our mission in America.''

''You have taken our money. You know I have established also an account for you in a Swiss bank. My mission is far more important, my Sikh comrades, than the pursuit of money. I know the value of money in helping you establish the independent state you wish. But only through armed revolution will what you want be possible. By that, I mean I am in the process of laying the groundwork for the seizure of the Indian parliament. But only after I have built up my force to the point where I am assured of success. You only need to know I, too, will honor my commitment to you. However, should you intend to walk out on me now, it would not be good. I would suggest you remain loyal to me.''

Adjan put steel into his voice. "Is that a threat, Major?"

"No. Let us just call it…sound advice."

"Are you forgetting, Major Slobovka," Adjan said, "that we lost several of our own Sikh brothers in America? They were good men. They wanted an independent Khalistan the same as we do, and they left behind wives and children. I hope their blood was not shed in vain."

"Now who is threatening whom?"

"No threat," Adjan countered. "We have proved ourselves capable warriors. If that was your intention by sending us to America, then the evidence speaks for itself. But we have no intention of being either your cannon fodder or suicide troops."

"I have never implied such a thing. I have gone through great risk to recruit, to train you here in this hellhole at the end of the world. The mere fact that you returned safely to India shows my faith in you, shows that I have a specific purpose for you in mind. I needed to find out quickly who and where my enemies are. I do not need my enemies yapping like hyenas at my heels when I initiate my final operation."

Adjan's gaze narrowed. "I am beginning to believe we served our purpose to you. Our trail from America was certain to be picked up by your enemies and lead them to the Punjab."

"There is some truth to that. What you were assigned to do was both a test of your reliability and necessary means to draw forth my enemies. I have uncovered three men who have sought to betray us.

Come. I want you to see just how serious I am about our endeavor.''

Slinging an AK-47 over a shoulder, Slobovka led the Sikhs and his commandos out into the bitter cold. Pulling up the hood of his fur-lined white parka, the major gave his surroundings a quick search. A solitary klieg light in the gorge revealed a heavy white mist had descended over the base. During the day, Slobovka recalled how that same mist cloaked the towering granite sawtooth ridges of the Himalayas. The snow was at least a foot deep. Earlier, when returning safely to the base, he had scanned with growing concern the break in the shroud of mist, noting the sky had been a threatening, low-lying sheet of gunmetal gray, nearly sitting on top of the mountains. He hoped the storm would hold off long enough for him to make the necessary final arrangements for safe passage to their secondary base in Tajikistan if a suitable glacier couldn't be found.

Trudging up the mouth of the gorge, Slobovka found the three Sikh traitors surrounded by six of his Spetsnaz commandos. In the glare of light, he read the ferocious hatred in the eyes of the three prisoners. The major stopped, turned and showed Adjan and Maraka a grim smile.

''If a man is to succeed, he must know who his enemies are, as well as his allies, and he must have the will to deal with each accordingly. These men are from a neighboring village near your home. Since I have come here, I have worked my own informants within the villages. They go about their lives as normal, but they have reported to me any Sikh who wants to undermine me or turn us in to the Indian authorities. These three were set to run to the military. I understand they have provided information to certain Americans who were interested in what we were doing here. I suspect these Americans are CIA, perhaps even the same armed force that is now marching for our position.''

When Slobovka smiled at the traitors, one of the Sikhs spit at the major's feet. Without hesitation, Slobovka unslung the AK-47 and fired a long burst, the stream of 7.62 mm slugs drilling into the trio's legs. Blood gouted from their shattered limbs, jagged shards of gleaming bone, as white as the snow, jutting through shredded cloth. The Sikhs toppled, the snow soaking up their flying blood, turning crimson. To Slobovka's amazement, the men didn't scream, only grunted. Obviously they had already accepted their certain violent end. Hate-filled eyes sought out Slobovka. One of the Sikhs turned the expression on Adjan and Maraka.

"You have become the lapdogs of your Russian masters. Do you not see? They will bring not only death and destruction to India, they will annihilate the Punjab. There will never be a free Sikh state of Khalistan!''

Slobovka emptied the clip into the Sikhs, driving them, twitching, deep into the snow. The major turned, his expression as hard as the Himalayan rock, and said, "I will not tolerate treachery, from any side, not even my own." Slobovka wasn't sure how to read the stony expressions on Adjan's and Maraka's faces, but he made a mental note to watch the men closely from there on.

He smiled coldly, then added for good measure, "A soldier of mine who does not perform his duty will die, slowly and in great pain if I have the time. After all, I have a reputation to uphold as Ivan the Terrible."

IT REMAINED TO BE SEEN what else the agent had neglected to tell him, but Bolan was prepared for anything. Should any more "by the way" scenarios pop up, Bolan decided he might cut out on the man. Brognola had briefed him about the Spetsnaz angle, but given that the GRU had set up shop in India, Bolan had already factored in the Russian commandos who came under the control of Russian Military Intelligence. It was the exact number of crack commandos the soldier strongly suspected he would eventually face down that he needed hard intel on.

One thing at a time. First the rendezvous with the SVR contact. And that alone activated the Executioner's radar for treachery.

From the airport, they had taken a cab into the heart of Old Delhi. Only moments earlier, Shiva had paid the driver. Now Bolan and his questionable partner were legging it down the shadowy but bustling bazaar of Chandi Chowk. Surging toward the lights of the hotel, which Shiva had informed Bolan would be their rendezvous site with the SVR contact, the soldier kept up hard surveillance on his flanks. The hustlers, vendors and beggars were out in force, even at that late hour. Ahead, Bolan spotted the marbled dome of a good-sized mosque. Side by side, the mosque and the hotel were swathed in soft light, ominous beacons, it seemed, lost and alone in the bowels of Old Delhi's midnight madness.

For a fleeting moment, the Executioner had the distinct impression his presence was being monitored from the southern gate of that mosque. In the next heartbeat, he was sure of it as the three shadows who seemed to be keenly interested in the two strangers with duffel bags over their shoulders, vanished beyond the gate. One moment they had been there, and the next they were gone.

Trouble, no doubt.

But a slew of ominous questions had nagged Bolan since his tense exchange with Shiva. Undoubtedly the soldier could trust no one, take nothing for granted. It would appear that there were many factions on both sides, SVR and CIA alike, scurrying all over India with their own agendas.

Bolan's goal was simple—hunt down the terrorists who had murdered innocent Americans, flush out the conspiracy, either foe or so-called friendlies, who had made the slaughter possible. Beyond that, the soldier would search out the roots of the conspiracy. Given all he had seen and been through since his deadly encounter with Sanjay Bahjwani in the restaurant bathroom, Bolan was certain some power was pulling the strings from the shadows. It was the idea of a joint SVR-CIA conspiracy that disturbed him the most. With renegade factions of the two most powerful Intelligence agencies in the world working together, entire nations could be in danger of being undermined, hurled into revolution and anarchy. If that was even their objective.

A slender figure boiled out of the shadows of an alley. Right away Bolan was digging inside his bomber jacket for the Beretta when Shiva laid a hand on his arm.

She stepped out of the shroud of darkness, walked right up to the CIA operative. Instinctively Bolan knew she was their contact. Dressed in black khakis and a dark windbreaker with the bulge of a holstered weapon plainly visible, she looked Bolan dead in the eye, as if measuring him for some hidden motive. He read the coldness in her almond eyes, which seemed out of place with her blond hair and ivory skin. The lady was a killer. Suddenly Bolan trusted the situation less than ever.

"Everything under control with the guru?" Shiva asked.

"We must hurry. I believe I have been followed. This way."

So much for introductions, Bolan thought, hesitating, sensing danger from some undetermined source. Shiva gave the Executioner a hard look over his shoulder, then Bolan followed as the SVR agent led them into the murky gloom of an adjoining alley.

No sooner was he surging down the alley than headlights hit Bolan's back. Whirling, he spotted the Volkswagen, barreling into the alley.

The Executioner glimpsed the startled anger on the faces of Shiva and the woman, but he was already galvanized into combat mode.

Three shadows burst out of the vehicle, armed

with assault rifles. Like wraiths boiling out of the night, tall and holding their ground beyond the thin curtain of white light, they swung AK-47s into full view.

Bolan had come into the situation, knowing anyone and everyone was a potential enemy. In the next eye blink, darting out of the glare of the headlights, the soldier acted on that ominous gut feeling. The Desert Eagle fisted and sweeping into target acquisition, the Executioner pounded out the first peal of rolling thunder just as the unknown enemy unleashed a triburst of autofire.

5

Bolan's grim concern was twofold. First there was the unknown enemy, blazing away with AK-47s the instant the threesome burst from the Volkswagen. Second there was the chance that his shaky alliance with the SVR agent and the CIA agent could suddenly blow up in his face.

The immediate danger was obvious, and the Executioner went to lethal work.

Chips of stone sparking above his head, Bolan hit a combat crouch and followed up his first shot, seeing his opening round had struck the enemy but had left him standing. Another peal of Magnum thunder, and the driver took the soldier's .44 hollowpoint round dead center in the chest. This time a crimson mist settled over the hood of the Volkswagen, drifting through the headlights in a fractured pink curtain. Before the Executioner's first kill took to the air, the other enemy ambushers were hurled back on their faces, in the most unforgiving terms.

In the next several heartbeats, Bolan let his second concern play out. If he had been led into a trap, with his new "allies" choosing to swing their weapons on him, then the Executioner would be ready to blast them into oblivion.

But it appeared exactly what it was for the moment, an ambush being fought off with all the deadly skill and cold ferocity of Bolan's unlikely partners.

Tracking on, the soldier triggered another round. Out of the corner of his eye, he glimpsed the crouched shadows of his allies. Shiva was sweeping a steady burst of 9 mm parabellum rounds from a mini-Uzi while the Russian pumped out one 7.62 mm round after another from a Tokarev pistol.

Glass exploded into the faces of the two surviving attackers on the passenger side, and there was a scream as razorlike slivers ripped into the second attacker's eyes. Throwing his hands up over his bloody mask, he didn't have to worry long about being blinded by glass needles.

Combined overkill from the triple barrage of the Desert Eagle, mini-Uzi and Tokarev shattered the air around Bolan. The blind became the savaged dead, his torso opening under the furious return fire as he was lifted off his feet, driven down the length of the Volkswagen. The third attacker attempted to streak for the cover of a doorway near the mouth of the alley, firing wild bursts from his AK-47 on the run.

The sole survivor never made it.

Intending to bag a prisoner, Bolan lifted the enemy off his feet with a well-placed thigh shot that carved off a ragged chunk of flesh. A hideous shriek knifed the gloom as the enemy slammed facefirst into the stone wall.

"I want him alive," Bolan rasped.

The Russian agent either wasn't listening, didn't care or was too pumped on adrenaline. As the Executioner slid out of the shadows, the Tokarev bucked slightly in her tight two-fisted grip, and three slugs cored into the head of the man Bolan wanted alive.

Slowly, with a bellyful of bad instinct and ice-cold anger, Bolan strode toward the woman, who cracked a fresh clip into the Tokarev.

"You either didn't hear me, lady," Bolan growled, "or you don't give a damn. But next time I speak, you better listen."

The woman's eyes were lit with the excitement of postcombat adrenaline. "I do not know who you are, but there is no time to be holding hands with wounded prisoners."

Shiva stepped in. "This is Colonel Pollock—he's with me."

"That tells me nothing."

"If I trust him, you can trust him, Agent Ulyatin."

"I trust no one," she said. "And do not use my name again."

"Before we go any further, I want to know what happened here," Bolan stated.

"It is simple," Ulyatin replied. "Those men were Spetsnaz assassins. Whether they have already executed the Sikh you came for, not to mention my own agents or the CIA operatives guarding him, we will see."

Bolan kept his steely gaze fixed on the woman. "You can tell they were Spetsnaz just by a quick look at three dead men?"

"I know. That is enough. Quick. The safehouse is not that far. We have no time to argue."

She was moving away when Shiva told Bolan,

"Just go with the program for now, Colonel. You'll get your answers in time."

"Why don't I feel comforted by that?"

"Let's shake a leg, Colonel. The Indian police won't take kindly to us shooting up the neighborhood a half hour after we're in-country. We'll be detained even if we are sanctioned—you can bet on that."

"Earlier, you made it sound like the Indian authorities don't care what we do as long as the right people get killed. That's how I'm going with the program from here on. The right people get killed, no matter what flag they hide behind."

Shiva threw the warrior an uncertain look. The Russian agent rounded a corner at the end of the alley, calling back for them to hurry.

The Executioner fell in, keeping combat senses locked on full alert.

THE SAFEHOUSE PROVED a slaughterhouse, but Bolan had expected to find it that way.

The room was at the end of what appeared to be a one-story apartment complex, three blocks north of the alley killzone. In that part of Old Delhi, torches and lanterns were still preferred over electricity. The lighting in the hallway had shadows dancing all around the Executioner.

Desert Eagle fisted, he picked up the rear, alert to any sound out of the ordinary, any sudden move by the Russian agent and the CIA agent. In the soft yellow flicker of the hallway's torchlight and lanterns, Bolan looked over their shoulders at the butchery, trying to observe the pitiless expressions of his companions as they took in the massacre. Dispassionate professionals or coconspirators?

At least a dozen crumpled bodies, awash in blood and gore, lay in the confines of the small Spartan room. There were at least four victims heaped in one corner, their wine-colored turbans and white beards, now stained crimson, identifying them as the Sikh guru and his entourage. Their age was impossible to put a finger on, since their faces had been riddled by so many bullets there was nothing left but slick pulp. Of undetermined nationality, the rest of the victims had taken one or more rounds through the chest. For slaughter of this size to take place, Bolan suspected several things. He voiced his suspicions, attempting to get a read on the Russian agent.

He addressed Ulyatin. "How many people other than yourself knew about this place?"

"No one."

"That you are aware of."

She hesitated, but relented. "*Da.* That I am aware of."

"Well, they knew their killer or killers."

Ulyatin turned her merciless expression on Bolan. "I can assure you it was not me."

The Executioner wasn't convinced. "The killer or killers came in with silenced automatic weapons to take out this many so quick. Maybe it was the three Spetsnaz gunners we ran into, could be somebody on either side you're working with. The killer or killers using silenced weapons might have bought us some time. For damn sure, if they had made the kind of noise we did back in the alley, this place would be crawling with the local authorities by now.''

"You seem very sure of things, Colonel," the woman said in a skeptical tone. ''But seeing the way you fought only a few minutes ago, I would say you are a warrior with some experience. Perhaps I have misread you. Perhaps your help and experience I will value.''

Bolan wasn't about to be swayed by any attempt at flattery or guile. "The only thing I'm sure of is we need to get out of the city. The second thing I'm certain of is that I'm going to get some straight answers once we're clear of Delhi.''

Shiva and Ulyatin looked at each other for several moments. In their silence, they seemed to be trying to reach some critical decision.

Finally Ulyatin spoke to Bolan. "Very well. We will talk, open and frank, but once we leave. I have a vehicle, secured and waiting for us just outside of the northern outskirts of the city.''

Bolan gave the woman room to pass.

Ulyatin glanced at the hand cannon, an odd smile on her lips. "You needn't concern yourself that I am the enemy, Colonel.''

"If you don't mind," Bolan said, looking from Ulyatin to Shiva, "I'll be the judge of that.''

Ex-CIA PARAMILITARY operative Judd Langston followed Special Forces Major Thornton in lockstep toward the four Huey gunships and the trio of Apache attack choppers. The hood of his white parka up, Langston took in the action of the joint Special

Forces–CIA paramilitary units moving to board the choppers, while his own force of twenty men split up to ride with the ground-attack teams in the white-camouflaged Land Rovers.

Operation Red Octopus was going down, but it wouldn't play out the way Major Thornton had planned, Langston knew. Somehow the former Company paramilitary operative kept the smile off his lean, heavily bristled face. It would be real simple, he thought, to swing the M-16 off his shoulder now and bury the major. Maybe too easy. He was under orders from the Council, though, and when the time came the Special Forces major would know something had gone terribly wrong, that Major Hank Thornton was on the losing side.

The spearhead of the ground force was already pulling out, kicking up fragile puffs of snow as the Land Rovers skidded past the northern edge of the Sikh village. During the major's final brief, Langston had convinced Thornton his team would be put to better use if they rode with the ground force. Thornton agreed, since Langston's reconnaissance had proved invaluable in pinning down the Spetsnaz base, since Langston knew the terrain near the gorge of the Himalayas and claimed he was an experienced mountaineer.

What the good major didn't know was a lot. For starters, Langston had neglected to mention a legitimate CIA strike force was en route to link up with the Special Forces unit. If and when the real CIA force rolled onto the scene, Langston knew he would have a major problem to confront. Whoever Langley had sent via its pipeline through the Pentagon, well, he knew they would spot him as a renegade. His cover, he knew, could only hold up so long. Luckily his liaison for the organization had enough clout and enough connections to infiltrate him into this clandestine commando operation, intercept and confirm radio messages about the real strike force through their own counterintelligence network.

Just beyond the rotor wash of his Huey, his slate gray eyes and bulldog face turning on the CIA operative, the major said, "All right, Langston, by the numbers. Dawn is still a good seven hours away. Plenty of time for us to get into position. Once your team is in place, a quarter klick from their gorge, you move in, no radio messages. We need to be in sync, you know the appointed hour. A coordinated ground-air assault. Once we fly in, we'll pour it on, give them enough death from above to make those Russian bastards wish they were back in Moscow with a bellyful of vodka. I want those Hinds blown up into scrap, with not even a chance for the Russkies to get them in the air. You people pinpointed the exact location of their hardsite. According to your recon, those Hinds and the two Antonovs are forty klicks due east of the gorge, neatly camoued on one fat flat plain. One strafe, they'll never know what the hell hit them."

The major was a fool, Langston thought. "Understood, sir. But you understand my orders, as well, I hope."

"I know all about what Langley wants, mister. You want one Ivan who calls himself the Terrible.

I'll go out of my way to see you get your man, but we're on the Indians' clock. If we don't clear Spetsnaz off the Himalayas in twelve hours, the Indian army moves in. That'll mean we've got one hell of a messy international incident in Uncle Sam's face.''

"Very well, Major. And good luck," Langston said.

Once the major hopped into the Huey, the CIA agent swiftly headed toward his Land Rover. He smiled as he caught the hard but laughing eyes of his men waiting for him.

The ghost of years gone, the sum total of countless operations just like this, from Southeast Asia to the bogus drug wars in South America, suddenly wanted to flash through Langston's mind. But yesterday was dead, and every day was a new day to look toward the future of a New World Order. It occurred to him right then, more than ever, that when a man thought he was strong, in control, like Major Thornton, he was truly vulnerable, truly at his weakest.

Langston met Al Martin's steely gaze. "Let's roll, gentlemen. This is going to be so easy it's damn near frightening."

"I trust everything is set to fall," Martin said.

Langston looked back over his shoulder as the gunship armada lifted off. "Like dominoes. Today India, tomorrow Russia. Next month, hell, who knows, we might be sitting in the White House, telling the unwashed masses of America just what it is we expect of them."

Langston piled into the vehicle and took the wheel. He couldn't help but chuckle, thinking the good guys never really stand a chance. Darwin was right, he thought.

Only the strong survived.

It certainly helped if a man was just a little bit tougher, a little bit smarter than everybody else, he believed. It was the kind of attitude that had seen him through the specter of all those years when doing the Company's dirty and wet work.

This time, though, the dirty work was for himself. The Council had promised him the world, and he would damn well make sure they delivered.

BOLAN SAT IN THE BACK of the Land Rover, with Shiva. Ulyatin drove the vehicle. Two hours out of Delhi, rolling north on a paved highway toward the Punjab capital city of Chandigarh, and the three of them stayed on edge. Frequently, as they moved on into the night, passing gloomy, low-lying stone dwellings, mosques and temples, the highway occasionally choked with bikes, rickshaws and rusty hulls of dilapidated vehicles, the three of them searched the highway, front and rear. So far so good, meaning they were moving with no sign of a tail, either faceless enemy or the Indian military or police.

Bolan's Uzi was out and by his combat boots. Behind the soldier, there were enough ten-gallon fuel cans to get them to the Pakistan border with plenty to spare.

Ulyatin glanced in the rearview mirror, her gaze sharp but softening a little as she met Bolan's stare. "All right, Colonel, we talk now. I would first like to say that there is much I am sure you either do not know about what is happening in India, or you have arrived at certain conclusions that could prove dangerous but only to you.''

"My objective is very simple, that's what I want to make clear before you go on. Just in case you were wondering, I want the ones responsible for going to America and killing innocent citizens. If those Sikh terrorists were trained and financed by a joint CIA-SVR conspiracy, then I go right for the head of the hydra—wherever it leads.''

"There is a conspiracy, Colonel," the agent said, "one that is so grave, with such potentially devastating worldwide implications, that, unless it is destroyed and quickly, I am afraid my own country could be thrown into a revolution that would in effect seal our borders and see an internal conflict that may push the world to the brink of war.''

"Why don't you start at the beginning. Who and what are these conspirators?" Bolan asked.

"I only wish I knew them by name. That would make my job, our job, that much easier. I am not sure what my CIA contact here has told you.''

She looked at Shiva, and the man gave her a quick brief.

Ulyatin nodded. "It is as he said. I can further tell you, though, that our intelligence sources have learned there is a plan to seize the Kremlin by force and install a new president of Russia, one who is anti-West and pro-Communist, the likes of which could make Stalin laugh with sadistic joy from his grave.''

"I'm getting some real mixed and bad signals

here," Bolan said. "One minute you tell me the left hand doesn't seem to know what the right is doing, the next minute you're hinting you know exactly what is going on. Which is it?"

"It is a little of both." Ulyatin showed Bolan a strange smile. "Welcome to the world of espionage."

"I've been there before. Everyone talks out of both sides of the mouth, and even if you had a scorecard you couldn't tell who the players are."

"Couldn't have said it better myself, Colonel," Shiva said.

"What's the bottom line here?" Bolan wanted to know. "Spetsnaz numbers, for starters."

"Eighty commandos, we believe," Shiva answered.

Ulyatin clenched her jaw. "But it could be as many as a hundred. Not to mention the Sikhs Major Slobovka has 'employed.' It could be as many as two hundred."

"And our side?"

"My strike force numbers twenty-four men."

Bolan let out a soft whistle. "That's only two squads. We'll be facing some long odds."

"Don't forget, Colonel," Shiva added, "We are to link up with a Special Forces commando team. You can tack on another sixty heavily armed professionals, plus a miniarmada of Hueys and Apaches. We'll be flying to rendezvous with a Major Thornton in two Hueys waiting with my people. There's going to be a full-blown war in the Himalayas before this is over. However, the Indian government does not want another Afghanistan on its hands. But if we don't resolve the situation quickly, the Indian military, one of the largest in the world, by the way, is set to move in and take matters into their own hands. That would prove an international fiasco. Right now official India, the government and its own Intelligence agency, will try to do their damnedest to keep this under the rug. Meaning they don't want an internal revolution starting in the streets of every major Indian city. You can imagine the panic when Indians start hearing, 'The Russians are coming.'"

"The Russians are already here. And you've already got a fiasco on your hands," Bolan said. "The Punjab is under a state of siege, whether the Indians want to go public with that or not."

"So let's make sure this doesn't blow any farther south or even north than the Punjab," Shiva said. "Full-scale war along the bordering countries will make Pakistan, Afghanistan, the Nepalese, even the Chinese, real nervous."

"Why was the Sikh you people were sitting on so important?"

"Again, politics," Shiva said. "First the guru had infiltrated his own informants into the Spetsnaz operation. Soorboka had hard intel on the numbers, the site, the hardware. Beyond that, he was to be a puppet buffer between any revolutionary Sikh factions left when the dust settled after this and the Indian government."

"So much for politics," Bolan commented. "I'll ask you once more what you know about this supposed superconspiracy of a renegade CIA-SVR alliance.''

Ulyatin seemed to ponder something for a moment, her expression dark. "What our own legitimate SVR-CIA alliance has learned is that the opposition is comprised of powerful former intelligence agents and directors of not only our respective agencies but of other intelligence agencies, as well. The Israeli Mossad, for example, the Iranian SAVAK. They have pooled their knowledge, their money, their connections and expertise to form a secret organization intent, it would seem, on overthrowing whole countries. *Da*, it is madness, but we have already seen just how serious, how capable they are. Perhaps they are even getting official support by our respective intelligence agencies. They are selling death, plain and simple. They want direct anarchy, but they will pull the strings of the revolution. Power and domination, Colonel—that would appear to be their obvious goal.''

Bolan directed his grim words at Shiva. "It somehow all goes back to what your specialist buddy told me in Virginia. This thing of yours has been building in the shadows for years. Financed exclusively, I imagine, by drug money and arms trafficking.''

"Sad to say, Colonel, you couldn't be more right.''

"I'm not in this looking to be right.''

There was a hard pause, then Ulyatin said, "Is there anything else you wish to know, Colonel?''

"Yeah. How much farther until we get to where we're going?''

Shiva took a few moments, looking at the illuminated dial of his watch, then studying his grid map with a penlight.

"I'd say 250 kilometers, Colonel."

"And your people know we're on the way?"

"They're expecting us. And they'll sit tight until we arrive, if that's what you're worried about."

Bolan grunted, letting that one ride. Something warned him his troubles had only just begun. The same gut instinct kept telling him he would be the only one watching his back.

MAJOR SLOBOVKA WAS pleased. First a suitable glacier had been found to hide his Hinds. At the moment, hands clasped behind his back, he scoured the dark, jagged ridges of the Himalayas, a wall of black ominous rock surrounding him, a stone ring providing the perfect fortress. Having moved to higher ground, they were now based somewhere between the Khyber Pass and the Karakoram Range. This was, for the most part, an uncharted region, so remote and inhospitable that either only a fool or an experienced mountaineer dared set foot in this part of the world. Or, Slobovka concluded, a warrior with a mission.

Second, and most important, he knew the enemy was set to attack at dawn, less than six hours away. His CIA counterpart was proving a worthy ally.

Trudging through the snow, Slobovka inspected the two magnificent ZSU-23-4s. The quad-barreled, 23 mm automatic cannons, capable of pounding out a lightning stream of high-explosive rounds in three-second bursts from each of the four cannons, were aimed east. That was the most likely direction from which the American gunships would attempt to swoop down on their mountain hardsite. The third antiaircraft cannon had left with the transport planes, which were hidden twenty kilometers east in a remote gorge.

Slobovka further inspected the area where he anticipated the battle would begin. Spetsnaz commandos were mere shadows, hidden in nooks or behind boulders, or crouched in the slivers of serpentine arroyos winding down the western edge of the glacier. Many of them toted RPG-7s, or the surface-to-air SA-7 Grail missile launcher. When the enemy came streaking over the glacier, Slobovka would be ready to blow them halfway into Pakistan.

A long klieg light bathed the sprawling glacier. Sliding into the outer limits of the harsh white light, Slobovka mentally put the tactics together. It was simple, in the way the Mongols under the Khans had slain whole armies—ambush, then retreat, draw the enemy into another ambush when that enemy believed you were on the run. Encirclement, annihilation. History had proved, right up to the defeat of the hated Germans, that sheer guts, determination, tenacity and willingness to die for the right cause would carry a soldier through, would indeed seal victory. When a man knew he was right, Slobovka thought, nothing could defeat him. And Major Slobovka, envisioning himself as the new savior of Mother Russia, knew he was right.

Still, there was much to be proved. First the American *kalorshniks* had to be defeated, or they would follow him like hungry wolves into Russia. It danced through his mind that he only wished he could be there when his ally led the unsuspecting American ground force into the abandoned tent in the mouth of the gorge. He would have liked to have seen the expression on the faces of the Americans when they saw what he had left behind. And who ever said, he thought, that the Russians were a people with no sense of humor?

Still, Slobovka wasn't about to take anything for granted.

Fortunately the weather seemed to be holding. But the reports from the base near the Afghan border had warned Slobovka that a paralyzing snowstorm, the likes of which had not been seen since 1941, had blanketed and gripped the endless steppe of his Motherland. Once again it appeared as if nature was conspiring against his cause. Once the American enemy was crushed in India, Slobovka would be forced to retreat to his secondary hardsite. Weather was weather, and he would deal with it. There was no other way.

The recruitment game had played out in India. Of course, he would continue to promise the Sikhs the world. After all, he would need them when the Kremlin was stormed. The Sikhs would be his spearhead, the front-line cannon fodder. They had been paid too much money to not follow through now, with the promise of more exorbitant sums to be delivered upon the seizure of the Kremlin.

Slobovka found Captain Petrov rolling up on his

flank. The captain saluted. "Comrade Major, our units are in place down the gorge, awaiting your orders. However, I am concerned about the Sikh units, their loyalty my primary concern."

Despite that news about the Sikhs, Slobovka was confident that the trap had been perfectly set. Petrov, he knew, like all Spetsnaz commandos, was trained to take the initiative. Slobovka already knew the sniper teams were in place in preselected sites on both sides of the gorge. Better yet, the lip around the glacier was mined. And the only way onto the glacier by foot was up the gorge. Surely the American strike force would find its way up the gorge, to the glacier. By then, it would be too late for many of them. Whatever enemy numbers were left standing would be picked off by his snipers with the high-powered Dragunov rifles. He had fought by Petrov's side so many times, Slobovka knew he could leave the captain and his commandos on their own to seek, engage and annihilate the enemy. The only questionable moment would come when they were attempting to reel in their CIA fish.

"Captain Petrov, let me make this as clear as possible. The Sikhs will fight. They will do as we want, because they have been paid—or we will kill them. We need them, but we do not need them that badly. They know what is at stake. Indeed, I intend to honor my pledge to them. They will have their Khalistan, even if it means we send in entire battalions to crush the Indian army. But first we must succeed in controlling our own country. I believe they understand that. However, keep a close eye on them."

Slobovka paused, smiling, admiring in the silence the sheer devastation he was soon to wreak on the American enemy. "My orders are simple. Our allies have informed us that we will be attacked at dawn. The ground force, however, is not to be attacked."

Petrov acknowledged the order with another salute, spun and moved off.

Alone, the major was tempted to ponder the future. A new glasnost was poised to stare the West right in the face. Only this time, Major Slobovka would be the power dictating all terms.

He was eager for dawn. Victory seemed assured.

IT WAS ALMOST FOUR HOURS later when they reached Shiva's command post.

According to the CIA agent, they were about forty miles due north of the Sikh holy city of Amritsar. The remote village of Hanjani, with its lanterns and drab stone dwellings and shuffling, shabbily garbed figures, seemed locked in eternal poverty. The only sign of modernization was the two Huey gunships, grounded beyond the walls of a Sikh temple.

As soon as they disgorged from the Land Rover, Bolan watched as dark-clad men toting M-16s with attached M-203 grenade launchers converged on Shiva.

"What's the status, Barber?" Shiva asked a tall, lean figure who raked Bolan with a cold gaze.

"We've got problems, sir. Something is very much AFU."

For some reason, Bolan wasn't surprised.

6

Even after Shiva gave his troops a quick introduction to Colonel Rance Pollock and Agent Lana Ulyatin, Bolan sensed they were neither trusted nor wanted. But that quickly became the least of anyone's problems.

They moved into a large hovel. The command center was equipped with only cots, a large radio console, radar screen and plenty of spare hardware, ranging from Ingram subguns to bundles of plastic explosive and LAW rocket launchers. Shiva shut the door, muting the howling wind outside.

Stamping snow off his boots, Shiva told Barber, "Let's have it."

Barber squared his shoulders. "We haven't been able to establish radio contact with Major Thornton. Just a dead line, not even static. Our radar shows air traffic to the northeast, and I'm assuming it's friendly. But since we were ordered not to link up with Thornton until you arrived, I can't say if it's us or them. They're flying all over the Himalayas like it's the holiday season at O'Hare. That's only the beginning. We've just received a report from our intelligence people that a group of renegade Company mercs has infiltrated the Special Forces unit. How, we don't know. Who exactly the renegades are we don't know, either.''

Shiva said nothing. Finally he looked at Bolan and said, ''Looks like we're going in cold, Colonel. We've got no choice but to make contact with Major Thornton, get him up to speed on what he's facing.''

''Everyone's on their own. Forget Thornton. If he's still alive when the sun rises, we'll think about him then.''

''Who's in charge here?'' Barber growled at Bolan, then looked at Shiva.

''We both are,'' Shiva said.

''I'm in charge of nobody but myself,'' Bolan countered. Then the soldier put a steely eye on Shiva. ''I guess I don't need to tell you we've got a potential full-scale snafu on our hands.''

An electric ripple of tension went through the room. Bolan held his ground. Before he even laid eyes on this strike force, the Executioner knew he would be the odd man out. Suspicions were confirmed, judging from the stony looks he received. More than ever, Bolan didn't trust the situation, and he fully intended to turn his guns on anyone on any side who even twitched a weapon his direction.

''We'll figure something out once we're airborne,'' Shiva said.

Bolan helped himself to a LAW rocket launcher. ''You don't mind, do you?'' the soldier said to Shiva. ''Looks like you can spare a few.''

Then, for the first time since their chat in the Land Rover, Ulyatin spoke up. Her voice was calm, but there was an edge of menace in her tone.

"One thing. This goes for everyone here. I want Major Slobovka alive. God have mercy on the man who kills him, either intentionally or in the heat of battle."

It would be simply another worry in a long list of concerns for Bolan. But whomever he cut down with his guns, it would be both intentional and in the heat of battle. He wasn't making any promises he couldn't keep.

"Let's get out of here," the Executioner growled.

He was the first one out the door into the icy cold. Dawn, he figured, was a mere couple of hours away. And as cold as the mountain air was, the soldier could feel the heat of battle, and treachery, already slamming him full in the face. For damn sure, he knew he would be walking into a free-fire zone.

If he was being sucked into the ultimate trap, then he would go down with guns blazing. Ulyatin was right about one thing. God have mercy on somebody's soul.

Anybody who got in his way, that was.

But somehow, some way, he intended to walk on from this battle, roll on for the heads of the hydra of the international intelligence superconspiracy.

"MAJOR, I'VE GOT A VIPER in my gut that's trying to tell me we've got a situation on our hands."

They were lifting off from the plain where the Russian air armada was supposed to have been grounded. Major Thornton turned to look at Captain Gruber. There were plenty of tracks in the snow that told Thornton the Russian choppers and Antonovs had been there, but they had been moved. Where? Why?

"Get me the grid map, Captain. My hunch is Spetsnaz has moved to higher ground. A glacier, I'd bet. Pass the word on. I don't want my gunships flying up this wall of rock all bunched up. In fact, only two Apaches, our bird and one other Huey. The rest stay behind to await my further orders."

Gruber spread the grid map on the floorboard. In the dim yellow light, Thornton locked a moment's grim stare with his captain. The major didn't like the doubt, the suspicion he read in Gruber's eyes. Something did indeed feel wrong. What, Thornton wasn't sure. He picked through his mind quickly, tried to get a handle on the source of his agitation. He recalled how only two days earlier the CIA strike force had shown up, on the heels of an official-looking Langley type with all the right credentials, paperwork, even signed orders from the Pentagon. Since this was a clandestine paramilitary operation, Thornton and his strike force were on their own, cut off from any official lines of communication with either Langley or the Pentagon. Their strike force was almost, but not quite, as secret as the GRU tried to keep Spetsnaz. From time to time, the Russians were forced to admit Spetsnaz existed. If the powers-that-be back in Washington couldn't keep the lid on what Special Forces was doing in India, heads would be rolling all over Capitol Hill.

Gruber went to the cockpit to radio the orders. Before he pored over the grid map, Thornton checked his watch. At that moment, Langston and the ground force would be moving into the gorge. Why did that suddenly bother him so much? the major wondered. The specialist had sworn his recon was tight, no chance they were spotted by Spetsnaz, no chance the Russians had anything that even resembled an antiaircraft battery, either. Suddenly Thornton wasn't so sure about the CIA people assigned to his strike force.

The major found what he was looking for, stabbed the map, and said, "Right here. This glacier. Pass the word on. I want my top guns locked on in an eye blink."

"Should I radio the ground team, get them up to speed on the situation?"

"That's a negative, Captain. No radio contact that could be intercepted by the opposition. We need to find those enemy gunships and disable them. If we don't, we're in a world of hurt."

"HEY, WHAT THE HELL is this?"

Langston fought to keep the smile off his face as an outraged Lieutenant Poole led the ground force into the large and obviously very abandoned tent. A dark scowl cutting the chiseled features of his young, handsome face, Poole stood with the other Special Forces commandos, as still as stone. They were all inside the tent, Langston saw, all of them packed together, glowering at the American flag, planted right in the middle of the floor.

But the flag was only the beginning of the message some comedian had left behind. A Russian funny man, damn right, and Langston knew exactly who the comedian was. Not too shabby a display, Langston thought. He'd buy the guy a round when we hit Moscow.

For starters, the comedian had draped a woman's skirt, bra and panties over the flag. Amused, Langston watched the young hotshots stew in their ire and indignation as they stared, grumbling and muttering curses at the sight of the two large black-and-white posters flanking the flag. One poster had the Chief Executive, with a large painted-on pipe, the type of device used to smoke dope, hovering around his lips. The other poster almost made Langston laugh out loud. The First Lady's head had been juxtaposed on top of the Herculean torso of a bodybuilder. The artist put the final touches of a mustache on the First Lady's face.

"I'd say our Russian opposition has quite the sense of humor," Langston said, chuckling. "Hell, I can see a right-wing talk show in the man's future."

Poole whirled on Langston. "You think this is funny?"

Langston ran a quick cold eye over his men, then let his gaze wander over the American flag patch on Poole's chest identifying the lieutenant as a friendly.

"Not at all, Lieutenant. In fact, things have gotten real serious. What's more, young soldier, you can take your naive patriotism straight to hell."

The deadly grim expression that hardened Langston's face caused Poole a long moment of confusion and paralysis.

In perfect sync with his mercs, Langston unslung and cut loose with his M-16. Poole took the first wave of blistering lead, the sweeping hellstorm of 5.56 mm slugs shearing the flag off his chest, chopping his white parka into bloody tatters. Before any of the Special Forces commandos could react, the mercs were scything down nearly a dozen of them, hammering bodies into one another.

It was a turkey shoot, Langston thought, holding down the trigger, ripping off hoods with sizzling lead that instantly blasted open skulls. Through the roaring din of relentless autofire, with screams of agony and grunts of surprise and rage lancing his senses, Langston held his ground, the M-16 chattering and blazing gory death at near point-blank range from his gloved fists. Within several eye blinks, bodies were twitching all over the ground beneath pooling streams of blood. Still some of the commandos fought back with savage determination, their training and discipline locked into their instinct for survival. Return fire from their M-16s sent several of Langston's men hurtling into the thick canopy, smeared with their showering blood.

Langston slapped a fresh 30-round mag into his M-16, darting to the side as several bullets drilled through the canvas behind him. Everyone was moving, dashing in all directions. There was enough light from the first rays of dawn for Langston to pick out targets on the run. Since his men were on one side of the tent and Thornton's people pinned down at the east edge, Langston didn't have to worry about catching one of his own mercs with an errant round. It meant Langston and his people could fire away, spray them with long wild bursts. It was one of the most hideous, but he had to admit to himself, most beautiful slaughters he had seen in years. Even as they died, Langston couldn't help but begrudge these young commandos some respect. But he had known all along they wouldn't go out quietly.

Finally, after long, flaming rakes of their combined autofire, Langston and company had cut down and gutted or damn near decapitated anything that moved in their gun sights.

In the deafening silence, Langston caught several low moans of pain. He found Poole crabbing through the scarlet-drenched hard-packed ground. Convulsing, blood spilling from his mouth, Poole reached out and tore down the flag.

"Why...you bastard...why?..." the lieutenant croaked, draped in the bloody Stars and Stripes.

Langston cracked a new mag home, chambered the first round. "For the money, son. What else? Hope you didn't think I was some kind of patriot."

With a grim chuckle, Langston drilled a 3-round burst into Poole's chest. Then the merc leader went to work on his own wounded, stitching 5.56 mm execution into his people. None of his men uttered even a grunt of protest. Everyone knew the drill. If you fell wounded, you died. No baggage. Standard Operating Procedure.

Unfortunately Langston found he'd lost six good men.

Moving outside, Langston got on his hand-held radio. He was already tuned into Slobovka's frequency. Looking up the dark mouth of the gorge, his men reloading and gathering around him, Langston stifled the laughter he felt roil in his belly. "This is Red-White-and-Blue to Big Bear, come in."

Static, then a long moment later, Langston heard the familiar voice of Ivan the Terrible. "Big Bear here. Status report?"

"Situation's under control. Have your people ready to greet us with open arms, Big Bear. We're coming home."

"Affirmative. We will be standing by to receive."

"Outstanding."

Signing off, Langston began the hard trek up the gorge. It occurred to him, more than ever, with a feeling of utter invincibility he hadn't experienced since he'd flown in three tons of cocaine for the Company to Miami, that he could do anything he damn well pleased.

And get away with it.

THEY CAME IN from the east, just as Major Slobovka knew they would. Only minutes ago, the radar had picked up and tracked their movement from the five-thousand-plus-foot peaks east of the glacier.

Slobovka barked the order for his ZSU fire teams to stand by. Already the Hinds and the two Mil Mi-8 assault transport choppers were lifting off, surging west behind a swirling wall of snow kicked up by rotor wash. Mere sight of his Hinds, Slobovka figured, should lure the enemy warbirds to the glacier.

The unsuspecting Americans would be blown out of the sky.

Securing cover behind a boulder at the west edge, Slobovka lifted an RPG-7, waited. Four shadows of gunships, cloaked in the broken skeletal fingers of the rising sun, banked in low, dwarfed by the towering walls of the Himalayas.

Slobovka lifted the RPG, drew target acquisition and roared, "Now!"

Just as the line of onrushing gunships broke the east perimeter, the two antiaircraft batteries pounded out a lightning stream of sizzling warheads. Miniguns and rocket pods flamed from the turrets of the American gunships for a brief moment, stitching lines of tracking lead and whooshing fireballs across the glacier, but the 23 mm barrage was already locked on for instant, pulverizing destruction.

A heartbeat later the sudden battle ended in abrupt annihilation for the four American gunships.

A smile started to crease Slobovka's lips. He was instantly heartened by the sight of roaring doom, the flash of fireballs raking the four gunships, the fleeting glimpse of the mangled shapes of men hurled from the flaming storm. Two gunships, tail rotors shot off, became whirling dervishes, colliding into each other. The rending of metal screeched over the glacier, bodies leaping or thrown from the fuselage by the impact. Fiery hulls seemed suspended in midair at the east lip of the glacier, then floated out of sight. Still, even as the sheet of blinding fire ripped over the glacier, armed figures kept leaping from the fuselage of one partially intact gunship. Spetsnaz autofire blistered the air as those shadows dropped beyond the glacier. There were a few screams, some midflight jerking as slugs ripped into their descending bodies. A final wave of thunderous cannon fire obliterated another gunship. Still, the GRU major

couldn't tell how many had managed to drop for the
cover of the gorge, which sloped away from the east
edge.

Slobovka pulled out his detonator box. The din of
cannon fire kept splitting the dawn asunder, shred-
ding the hovering warped wreckage of one remaining
gunship that appeared beyond the rippling firewall in
the sky.

Instinct and paranoia told Slobovka there would
be survivors. He ordered his men to move out.

Ivan the Terrible thumbed the switch, settled his
finger over the detonator button.

UZI IN HAND, Bolan hopped out of the gunship. Even
before he followed Shiva and the CIA strike force
into the tent, he knew what they would find. Ragged
bullet holes and the dark and already frozen plasters
of blood stuck to the canvas. Against the dawn light,
Bolan made out the twisted heaps of bodies beside
the flap, which was fluttering in the stiff, icy breeze.

Inside the tent, sprawled and shredded corpses littered the ground. Clenching his jaw, Bolan watched
Shiva inspect the dead. The soldier gave Ulyatin,
who held her ground by his side, a hard sideways
look. Everything felt so wrong to him. No one looked
surprised or suspicious. There wasn't even the hint
of outrage. He found nothing but stony expressions.
Just another day at the office.

The Executioner spotted the American flag patches
on many of the dead, a fireball of anger boiling in
his gut. He'd seen enough, glimpsed Shiva squatting
over a line of corpses near the edge of the tent. Whatever had happened here, the soldier knew a setup

when he saw one. Two opposing lines of dead men, each side with a Stars and Stripes patch. Death masks of bewilderment and outrage were on one side. On the other team he found only paralyzed faces of anger.

Bolan locked a gaze with Shiva, who stood and jerked a nod for them to step outside. The soldier held his ground, waited for the CIA agent to go first.

Outside, stepping away from the tent, Bolan took in their surroundings. The Hueys were kicking up slick sheets of snow beyond the tent of slaughter. Checking the gorge to the north, he saw the gloom was quickly being pierced by the threat of full-blown daylight. But a billowing plume of white mist had settled, five hundred yards or so up the gorge. From that direction, several of Shiva's men were surveying the snow. One of them informed Shiva maybe two dozen sets of tracks led up the gorge. The killers of the men inside the tent were up there, Bolan knew. Whatever else awaited them remained to be seen.

Ulyatin rolled up on Shiva's rear. "From the look on your face, I would say you know something."

Shiva looked grim and addressed both Bolan and the SVR agent. "I think we need to talk for a minute. I knew several of those men, or rather, knew of them. We've got a problem here."

Suddenly Bolan caught a faint but familiar sound of distant rolling thunder. It pealed on trailing waves down through the gorge. Everyone froze.

The Executioner knew a battle was raging somewhere to the north. "If you have something you want to say, I suggest we fly and talk. I have a hunch your Major Thornton just found Spetsnaz."

Again Bolan waited until Shiva boarded the gunship. If the agent didn't come clean about the slaughter they'd found, Bolan was prepared to take matters into his own hands.

Damn the odds. The Executioner would carry on the hunt. As far as Bolan was concerned, he was on his own.

A TIDAL WAVE OF SNOW and fire took to the air.

Slobovka stood, rooted in the middle of the glacier. Now he could smile. One thousand pounds of plastic explosive sheared the lip of the glacier as easily as a man with a razor-sharp knife would slice through soft butter. The earth beneath Slobovka trembled with awesome seismic force, and he watched as the flaming scrap of the final downed gunship vanished behind the white man-made mountain.

A deep rumble followed as at least one-quarter of the glacier peeled off. On soaring geysers of fire, a sheet of ice, snow and stone three times the size of a football field slid away from Slobovka.

Nothing, he knew, could survive an avalanche of those titanic proportions.

Slobovka radioed his Hinds and Hips back, then ordered a ten-man team to inspect the killing ground beyond the lip, just in case.

The major strode toward one of his gunships. It was time to hunt fresh game. The war, he suspected, had only just begun.

7

Everything had gone to hell. For Major Thornton, the sky had fallen; the world was coming to an end.

Or was it?

A soldier's soldier, who never expected the men under his command to perform a duty he wouldn't do himself, the major dredged up cold reserves of grim determination. Somehow he'd been spared. One second, they were sweeping in for the glacier, locked in on the Hinds, and then the sky had ripped open in a roar of thunder and blinding saffron flashes. Cannon fire. The goddamn spook, Langston. Whether he'd been set up, lied to and marched into a trap, Thornton couldn't be sure, and didn't really care at that moment.

First survival, then revenge.

Thornton would settle up with Langston later. Provided, of course, he lived through the next hour.

Stifling a groan, the major checked his limbs. He was cut and bloodied, but nothing was broken. It seemed that the midair collision had thrown him from the fuselage. From there, he'd hit the slope at an angle, cushioned by the deep snow, tumbled hard down the steep incline. Through a shattered haze, he'd seen the torn bodies of his men, severed limbs twirling through the air. He wasn't a believer in good fortune created by divine winds of fate, because a man made his own luck. But it fleeted through his mind that somehow the fickle gods of war had chosen to spare his life. He had rolled up beneath the cover of a jagged precipice, which had saved him from being crushed by the avalanche. Thanking his lucky stars, he recalled a sound louder than any artillery barrage or thunderstorm he'd ever heard. That was when the glacier erupted. The Russians had mined the lip.

After that, during free fall, darkness had gripped him with an impenetrable wall. How long had he been out? What the hell was the situation? For damn sure, it was grave any way it was sliced.

Sheets of thick snowdrift were still falling down the slope, telling the major he hadn't been out but for a few minutes at worst. Beyond his point of cover, Thornton saw the lifeless eyes, the bloody, shattered heads of his men jutting out of the snow. Here and there, an arm or a leg poked out of the mounds of white, stretching down the incline, which was littered with wreckage and more dead soldiers. Crackling flames then lanced his ears through the loud ringing, the stench of burning fuel and torched flesh triggering roiling nausea. Four downed gunships. He bit off the curse, choked down the rage. Ivan was up four-to-zip.

Thornton cleared the haze with an iron will. He heard voices up above, Russian voices, growling in their native tongue. The major hauled in his M-16 with its attached M-203 grenade launcher.

It was payback time.

THEY WERE AIRBORNE, soaring above the sawtooth peaks of the lower Himalayan chain, clinging to roughly eight thousand feet, Bolan had been informed by Shiva. But they had been flying northwest by the Executioner's order, soon to swing south, then to hit the ground on foot. That high up, it would be hard going. Frostbite, windburn and snow blindness, though, would likewise soon become the least of anyone's worries, the soldier knew. Full-scale war was about to be launched.

Altitude was both a problem and a solution. Since the enemy was using assault choppers, the ceiling would be ten thousand feet. Beyond that, the air would be too thin to keep any warbird in flight. That meant the enemy was entrenched, somewhere up the gorge, perhaps a glacier.

Before liftoff, the Executioner had laid out the battle strategy. The enemy had obviously marched up the gorge. To follow them into the gorge by gunship could mean getting blown to scrap by entrenched rocket teams before they knew what hit them. The idea now was to come in from behind the enemy from the northwest. Once Shiva's flyboys picked up movement with their heat-seeking radar, Bolan and the agent would disembark with their ground force. Shiva agreed it was the only logical tactical maneuver. The flyboys would be on their own, but at that point, everyone knew the score. Pour it on, roll the dice. Stand up, be counted. If death came for any man, he was to make sure he took out as many of the enemy as he could.

"Now, how about some answers?" the soldier asked, standing face-to-face with Shiva, the throbbing of the Huey's rotors filling his ears.

"I recognized four of those dead men. They were part of a group that I worked with years ago in South America. They were called 'the Butchers.' And for damn good reason. They were saboteurs, insurrectionists gathering intelligence for the Company, training rebels ostensibly. What they turned out to be was black marketers, attempting to foment unrest in the lower Americas, pretty much for their own personal gain, though they put the usual us-and-them slant to justify your basic murder, extortion. Mercenaries, but trained and hired by our side. I'm sure you've seen the type, Colonel."

"More than I care to admit."

"Anyway, I was called out of the operation, never told why, simply reassigned to some hellhole across the Pacific. I'm sure you can imagine the drill. Guns for drugs. The Company's own little dirty war, keep communism from getting a toehold on America's back door, in the meantime turn a fat buck. What Uncle Sam wanted was its own puppet regimes installed in certain sensitive countries, primarily the cocaine-producing Andean countries. Well, these guys worked out a whole lot better than the CIA had envisioned. Hell, they were so good, they damn near toppled at least two major nations in the lower Americas that I was aware of. The head merc's name is Langston. The Company gave him free rein to run wild down there, even turned him in the direction of any loose tongues back in D.C. who got wind of what was happening. Meaning the guy has no problem killing the players on our side. He disappeared several years ago once the big shots in Washington started lifting eyebrows, calling all kinds of people before Senate hearings. But what my intelligence arm has uncovered is that Langston has resurfaced and he's working with Slobovka. Langston's, in all probability, being bankrolled by this secret intelligence organization we're after. He killed those Special Forces commandos back there, most likely, I imagine, to shave the odds. Bottom line, it all tells me this organization we're trying to get to obviously has enough official clout to have infiltrated him into what was supposed to have been a legitimate clandestine operation to terminate Slobovka and his Spetsnaz force. In short, Major Thornton never knew what hit him or his people back there.''

''Was this Major Thornton among the dead?''

''No, but I'm sure Langston has worked out a plan with Slobovka to nail Thornton and the rest of his team.''

''How much more are you holding back?'' Bolan asked.

Shiva put a defensive edge to his voice. ''That's it, Colonel. You're up to speed.''

Ulyatin, an M-16 now slung across her shoulder, told Bolan, ''It is as we have been saying to you all along. We are asking for your cooperation, Colonel.''

Bolan said nothing, but they made a strong argument. They needed either Langston or Slobovka alive in order to lead them to this organization. Still, in the heat of what he knew was an upcoming battle, all bets would be off. The Executioner had enough names for the Stony Man computer wizards to fill in the gaps, track down even the shred of a lead that would get Bolan to this powerful clandestine organization.

One of the pilots suddenly called out from the cockpit. "I've got movement to the south, four klicks and closing. Just beyond those peaks. Air and ground."

"Find someplace to set us down. Get us inside one klick, if possible," Shiva ordered. "Ten minutes for us to make our approach, then proceed to make a wide sweep of possible target area. If a weapon is turned your way, hit them with everything you've got. At this point, I'm ordering you to blow anything that moves off this mountain."

"Sounds like you've given up on Thornton," Bolan said.

Shiva put a steely look on the Executioner. "Right now, Colonel, it's every man for himself. This is where we get off and leg it in."

Bolan didn't like the sound of that, but he understood the logic. Since every gun out there was tripping over itself, it was time to shoot first and ask questions later. But if Thornton was straight, and still alive, Bolan could find a potential ally in the major. After all, the major's soldiers had given their blood to the hands of traitors. If nothing else, that signaled Bolan the man could be counted on.

As soon as the gunship touched down, Bolan followed Shiva out the door into the cold air.

Locked and loaded, the Executioner moved out with the strike force in a skirmish line down a steep gully. In just a short while, the soldier had a grim gut feeling more of the truth would reveal itself. It was leaking out in pieces, with each passing hour.

In flesh and blood.

THIS TIME THE SNOW proved a deadly trap for the Russians. And Major Thornton decided there was something of a poetic justice in their tripping and stumbling down the incline. Three of the enemy sunk up to their necks in a snowdrift created by their own hand.

Peering around the corner, he counted ten Spetsnaz commandos in white camous and a white beret with what he believed was a red star. Silent white wraiths once they stopped cursing and snapping orders all over the place, they were sliding down the slope to the south. Having already checked his other flank, Thornton found the north ridge clear. With the sun having risen over the eastern peaks, a dazzling white light now blazed off the endless sea of white. To fight off snow blindness, the commandos wore dark-tinted goggles.

Being snow-blind, Thornton grimly determined, was about to become the least of their problems. He was hell-bent on blinding these bastards forever.

Just as Thornton slipped on his own protective goggles, the air was ripped by short bursts of AK-47 autofire. Several of his men had survived downslope and were crawling from flaming wreckage. Sharp grunts carried through the air as Thornton watched his wounded crucified into the snow.

Cold rage in his belly, Thornton drew target acquisition. The enemy was lined up, unaware, Russian rats in a row. Now.

Holding down the trigger, Thornton unleashed a long, stuttering burst of 5.56 mm lead that stitched the Spetsnaz commandos, flank to flank. Before they even knew what hit them, Thornton had mowed down five. White camous became pocked with ragged crimson holes, spurting blood across the snow. Alive with searing adrenaline, the major poured it on until there was nothing in white camous left standing. If they were mired in the snow, Thornton shattered their skulls, hurling beret, brain and gore down the slope.

Then the Hind loomed over the sheared lip of the glacier.

Without hesitation, Thornton triggered the M-203. The warhead streaked up the incline, zigzagged a flaming tail, then slammed into the turret of the warbird. As the Hind blossomed into a ball of hovering fire, Thornton cracked a fresh 30-round magazine into the M-16.

One last hard surveillance of the scene, listening intently, and Thornton didn't see anything move, didn't hear anything but the roar of fire then the hammering of wreckage.

He broke cover, started the grueling haul up the slope.

To his flank, the flaming hull of the Hind tumbled past his ascent.

One thing at a time, he told himself.

One battle down.

If nothing else, he'd cut the odds.

Make it four-to-one, he thought.

And there was still plenty of hell to pay.

FROM THE OPEN FUSELAGE doorway of his Mi-8, Slobovka saw the fireball erupt over the east edge of the glacier. He cursed, enraged over the loss of even a single Hind.

He began to bark orders to his pilots. His Hinds were flying low, south down the gorge, hugging the east face of the glacier until they went into a pre-ordered hover. Slobovka assessed his situation. The bulk of his Spetsnaz commandos and Sikh fighters were entrenched in the gorge, up and down the steep walls on both sides. They were waiting for further orders, prepared to greet their American counterparts, but they were also sitting targets. There was little doubt in Slobovka's mind that more enemy gunships were out there. But where? When would they show?

Slobovka decided to take initiative. He had abandoned the ZSUs too soon. He ordered his Hip and two other Hinds back to the glacier. Obviously some of the Americans had survived. Undoubtedly there would be others coming, on foot or by gunship. It was time to greet them when they came over the jagged lip of the glacier.

A moment later, much to his sudden horror, Slobovka saw two gunships burst out of the thick white mist to the north. Miniguns were flaming and rocket pods were chugging deadly payloads. Below, he watched as the enemy gunships tore through at least a half-dozen entrenchments of his Spetsnaz fighters. Bodies were cartwheeling through the air, and smoke, snow and stone washed across the gorge in a swirling blanket of destruction. Behind, Slobovka felt the aft of his transport assault chopper shudder against a tremendous explosion. A second later, he was informed by his pilot they'd just lost another Hind.

Then, as suddenly as they had struck, the enemy gunships banked high and to the west, vanishing beyond the higher ridges, out of range of rocket fire.

Slobovka barked the order to his pilots to get them back on the glacier but put two Hinds in pursuit of the enemy. He then told his pilot to order the ground force to move south down the gorge. Instinctively he knew the enemy would be sending in its own ground force from the north. Clever bastards. They had outplayed him, circling wide to the west, coming down on his rear, but their victory would only be for the moment. If he could get the invaders far enough down the gorge, he could bury them with another avalanche.

Of course, that might mean losing more than a few of his own men. But sometimes, Ivan the Terrible reasoned, sacrifices had to be made in order to achieve ultimate victory.

IT DIDN'T ESCAPE Langston that his Russian counterparts could turn on him. After all, he knew just how expendable a man could become once he fulfilled his end of a bargain or successfully completed his part of a military operation. Infiltration, annihilation, cut the odds. That was the deal he'd struck with Slobovka. Now Langston's part was finished, at least for the moment. Could be Slobovka decided he didn't need him anymore.

Marching point, his chest burning from the raw exertion of high-stepping through the foot-deep carpet of snow, Langston led his force to the outer limits of the heavy mist. Only minutes ago, he had heard the incredible rumble, a sound that seemed to split the blue sky, shake the earth beneath his feet with earthquakelike force. Slobovka had laid a trap, mined the glacier, maybe the gorge.

Sunlight glinted off something high to his left flank, and Langston swung his M-16 in that direction. Through his shaded goggles, he made out the red star, recognized the face of Captain Mikhail Petrov. The captain didn't look too eager to take that Dragunov off its mark. The muzzle was aimed right at Langston's chest.

"You mind pointing that rhino gun some other direction, Captain?"

A strange smile cut Petrov's lips. Silently Langston cursed. Smart-ass.

The Dragunov swung away, and Petrov called down, "Welcome back."

"What's the situation?" Langston asked.

"We wait for orders from Major Slobovka."

North, Langston spotted the Hinds sweeping off

the glacier. They flew low, then stopped, hovering over the gorge, kicking up walls of misty snow.

"What the hell was that thunder I heard?"

"It was the sound of victory."

"Jesus," Langston muttered. "You care to be more specific?"

"We mined the glacier. Your Major Thornton received an appropriate military burial."

Avalanche, Langston knew. How much more of the gorge was mined? Crazy Russian bastards.

Then it happened. At first Langston believed he'd been set up. Two gunships, Hueys, burst out of the wall of mist to the north. Miniguns were blazing and rocket pods were chugging away like there was no tomorrow. The first tracking line barely missed Langston as the merc nose-dived for the cover of a boulder. He looked back as the gunships swooped down, saw at least a half dozen of his men kicked off their feet by man-eating lead.

Langston looked up, ready to wipe the grin off Petrov's face forever. The Hind rearguard was already veering back for the glacier, but one of the gunships was blown out of the sky, descended in a slow, flaming spiral before impact. Petrov was on his radio, taking his orders, when Langston saw a fireball vaporize the Spetsnaz captain into something flopping to the gorge a moment later that wasn't even recognizable as human.

No setup.

Either Thornton or the latchkey CIA strike force was making its move.

Suddenly the two Hueys were gone, but two Hinds

were in pursuit. Dead men were hitting the gorge all around Langston, falling from their cover of caves and jagged overhangs.

From his cover, Langston ordered his men to higher ground. Then he found a Russian in his face.

"Major Slobovka has spotted a ground force coming from the north. We are to draw their fire, bring them this way."

"I'm not looking to dance around here, pal," Langston growled. "I want this finished, and I want to be on one of those Antonovs headed back for the safety of your Mother Russia."

"It is not that simple. We engage, then retreat. I suggest you move your men back and stay to the high ground."

It was then that Langston saw at least thirty shadows, leapfrogging down the arroyos and the crevasse to the north.

"Why's that?" Langston asked the goggled Russian.

"Because there will be an avalanche that will bury you and all of us if you do not move quickly."

He knew it. Langston gritted his teeth, barked the order for his men to engage in a fighting withdrawal. Damn right, it suddenly struck the man that he was expendable. It was the shoe on the other foot he didn't care all that much to be wearing. Well, if he lost any more men because Slobovka wanted the easy way out, he'd settle up with the Russian later.

He'd show the major just what selling death was really all about.

Wholesale. No bargain.

8

Shiva was barking orders to his commandos when Bolan decided to strike out on his own. Downrange, enemy corpses had piled up in the gorge, thanks to the sudden lightning strike by the Hueys.

It was far from being enough.

Their back-door-surprise advantage gone, enemy return fire was instant, vicious and heavy. A quick head count of the opposition, and the Executioner figured they were facing anywhere from fifty to seventy guns down there. The enemy appeared to be a mix of white camous, fur coats and turbans, a combined Spetsnaz-Sikh force. Long odds, even with another Hind out of the picture, the downed warbird now smoking and flaming in the middle of the gorge. Bolan had to believe that the butchers of innocent Americans were somewhere among the enemy they now faced.

"Colonel, you want to get with the program?" Shiva hollered. The agent and his commandos were hugging the west wall, firing, covering in three-man teams while another trio of flaming guns advanced at an enemy that was coming down from its high-ground entrenchments. "I need every available man here!"

Something looked and felt wrong to the Executioner about the engagement. The enemy was staging a fighting withdrawal, spraying wild autofire, lobbing off an RPG warhead here and there. Outnumbered by the enemy, it stood to reason that the Spetsnaz troops should either hold their ground or drive ahead, fire, cover, advance. Suspicious, right.

Looking up the slope from his northernmost point at the glacier, Bolan watched as the two Hinds and two bulky transport Hips swooped from the gorge, going in low, trailing funnels of snow. A heartbeat later, with the whine of lead hitting rock near his flank and the thunderclap of a Russian warhead hurling shock waves too damn close to his cover, Bolan saw the warbirds vanish.

Back to the LZ. But why? Bolan wondered. The sound of earlier thunder haunted the Executioner, pricked at ominous instincts. The gorge sloped, north to south. The west edge of the glacier was a thick sheet of ice and snow. And it ended at a point beyond which Bolan found the enemy retreating, at least six, maybe seven hundred feet of sheer snow and ice, sloping up from the gorge.

Bolan found Ulyatin by his side, the woman's eyes alive with fiery determination.

"Something tells me I should stick with the winners," she told Bolan.

The Executioner let it ride. It was every hunter for himself, damn right. If Ulyatin wanted to play hardball with his life, then Bolan determined he would have no compunction in cutting the woman down.

"Colonel!"

"I don't like what I'm seeing," Bolan called back over the relentless crash of autofire. "They want to draw us in."

"Bullshit. They're running and I'm going to chase them down, kick them right in the teeth," Shiva declared.

"You're on your own," Bolan called back.

"We'll settle up later, Colonel."

There might be nothing left to settle, Bolan suspected.

He moved out, found a point of entry toward the gorge, up a narrow crevasse. With Ulyatin right on his heels, the Executioner kept his grim gaze locked on the ridge above.

Razor-sharp combat alertness paid off. They came over the rise, eight white-suited commandos in all. The Spetsnaz force had gun sights fixed on Shiva and his men, were drawing target acquisition when the Executioner spewed 9 mm parabellum death.

With Ulyatin's M-16 streaming out lead doom beside him, Bolan hosed down the enemy soldiers, kicking them in all directions, bloody, dancing stick figures that never knew what hit their blindside.

Cracking a fresh clip into his Uzi, Bolan topped the rise, braced for anything.

He discovered the middle of the glacier was a flurry of activity. Maybe a hundred yards northeast, the two Hinds were hovering, securing the flanks of the grounded transport choppers as Spetsnaz teams disgorged. Quickly Bolan discovered the reason for the haste to get back to the glacier. Two four-man teams were racing for the antiaircraft cannons. A lone figure was strolling away from one of the transport choppers, his snarling voice carrying across the glacier on rotor wash.

The doomsday numbers were tumbling in Bolan's head.

"That's Slobovka," Ulyatin growled.

Bolan unsnapped the fiberglass LAW, lined up one of the Hinds in its death sights.

"What are you doing?" Ulyatin snapped. "I want Slobovka alive."

Bolan put a steely edge to his voice. "What you want is unimportant to me."

She looked set to swing her assault rifle around, but some of the fury faded from her eyes. "If you kill him, you will answer to me personally."

"What I said stands. Now, you want to help out or sit there and complain?"

It was then that more unexpected players entered the battle.

In the corner of his eye, Bolan spotted three gunships, streaking over the peaks to the south of the glacier, one Apache, two Hueys. The only logical conclusion was that the rest of Thornton's cavalry had arrived. Could be too little, too late, but the soldier knew they could use all that added firepower. If nothing else, an aerial dogfight could give him the distraction he needed to make an all-out fighting advance for the Spetsnaz gunships, bag the GRU major.

There was a sudden note of desperation in Ulyatin's voice. "Please, Colonel. I want Slobovka alive!"

Bolan didn't have time to argue. "So do I, lady.

I suggest you take out that bunch going for the cannon closest to us while I shave the odds.''

Bolan triggered the LAW.

As the tail of flame zigzagged on its lethal course across the glacier, locked on to a Hind, Ulyatin cut loose with her M-16, dropping three Spetsnaz commandos in midsprint for the cannon.

SLOBOVKA FOUND THEM under attack from all directions. He had just received word from his radioman that his force was, for the most part, out of range for the intended avalanche. Still, it was risky. Word was they had wounded, bleeding stragglers fighting desperately to climb the ledges higher up the gorge. If he blew the edge too soon and some of his wounded managed to survive, it wouldn't look good. Indeed, it would appear they had been sacrificed. There was no other way. It was critical they savaged what they could of the enemy, evacuate India by the Antonovs. Once inside the Russian border, he could contact the Council, await further orders, worry about the future from the safety of his secondary base.

The three enemy gunships came out of nowhere. Slobovka glimpsed his Hinds and the trio of enemy warbirds fire away at one another at almost point-blank range. Goggles on, AK-47 in one hand and the detonator box in a gloved fist, Slobovka found so much happening at one moment that in the confusion and chaos of battle it was impossible to decide whom to strike back at first.

Sliding beyond the rotor wash, icy wind and snow pelting his exposed face like a thousand needles, Slobovka lifted the AK-47 to return fire at two figures at the far northern edge of the glacier when divots began to erupt around his feet. Wheeling as yet another of his Hinds burst into flames overhead, Slobovka found one lone figure, crouched in the snow, cutting down his commandos with a chattering M-16.

Wreckage was slicing all around Slobovka, bowling down commandos to his flank in doomsday thunder and lightning. Just as he was about to spray the lone enemy near the east edge, one of the survivors, he suspected, of the earlier avalanche, a flaming hull collapsed at some point in front of the figure. Was that enemy crushed or covered by the debris?

With no time to wonder, Slobovka joined his force in directing countless streams of autofire at the attacking warbirds. From behind, cannon fire pounded the air. One of the Apaches veered off, but the other two gunships were obliterated. Still more tidal waves of raining scrap slammed the glacier.

Again, with autofire stitching the ground near his feet and flaming walls of scrap hurtling for his position, Slobovka nose-dived. Covering his head, he rode out the thunder, felt the slipstream of searing fire wash over him, even penetrating, it seemed, the double layers of thermal protection. Looking up, he found at least a dozen of his commandos pouring it on the two figures near the cannon. If the enemy got to that cannon first, he knew his choppers and his entire force would be blown right off the glacier.

Slobovka slid up on a knee, realizing he'd lost the detonator box. He starting sweeping the snow with angry strokes, when a bullet drilled into the ground, slashed a furrow across the fragile powder. The wild shot revealed what he wanted.

Without hesitation, the angry roar of the firestorm to his flank in his ears, the major grabbed up the box and thumbed the switch for activation. A cruel smile slashed his thin lips as he swiveled his head, looking westward.

This time would be even more devastating, he knew. Two thousand pounds. Twice the punch.

Slobovka hit the button.

SHIVA, WHOSE REAL NAME was Gary McNeary, was beginning to wonder if the operative handle he'd chosen, after the Indian god of death, would be flung back in his face.

The enemy troops were fighting like demons, on both sides of the gorge. Snarling masks of grim determination beneath white berets and turbans were popping up as the enemy force withdrew down the slope. Neither the Russians nor the Sikhs seemed to give a damn about the wounded. If you fell, you stayed. So be it. It was a tough life, and McNeary wanted it to get that much tougher on these bastards.

McNeary caught the distant but equally determined barrage of autofire and explosions from the glacier. Damn that Colonel Pollock, striking out on his own. McNeary needed his gun right then because he was losing men, right and left. They were outnumbered, and even as the enemy troops retreated they were catching his men with winging bursts of autofire. Firing, then sliding back, then scaling the wall. Yes, something looked suspicious to the CIA agent. The colonel's words were ringing through his head. But no, they weren't drawing them in; rather, the enemy soldiers were reeling them down while they went up the side of the gorge. Obviously the Russians and the Sikhs knew the terrain. What the hell was happening here?

And where were his gunships? McNeary wondered. With all the autofire and pealing of explosions sweeping over the gorge, it was becoming impossible to tell who was doing what to whom. Right then, it was indeed every man for himself.

Then it sounded and felt as if the whole mountain was about to come crashing down on his head. Looking up, McNeary was paralyzed by the terrifying sight of a two-hundred-yard gushing stretch of snow and fire leaping for the sky. There was a long rumble, the earth shuddering under his feet as if it might split open and swallow him whole. Then McNeary and his men scrambled for cover, any hole, nook or crevice they could find. They looked like cockroaches in his narrow field of fear-edged vision, skittering from a sudden burst of light.

McNeary knew what had happened—worse, what was coming.

Pollock had suspected a trap, and the man had been right.

McNeary wanted to curse the man's good fortune but figured Pollock had his hands full at the moment, if he was even still alive.

But the world was roaring down on Gary McNeary, a sea of descending white, gaining instant, furious life in one horrendous slide, threatening to crush him with tons of snow, rock and ice in the next few moments. Perhaps his last seconds on earth, he angrily thought. The irony of it was that he also heard a self-mocking voice tell him he'd chosen the wrong handle for this operation.

If he got out of this one, he decided he might listen to Pollock next time.

IF THE ENEMY FOUGHT with a sense of rage and desperation before, Bolan now found his adversaries coming at him with a suicidal, demonic fury.

The Spetsnaz commandos became automatons hell-bent on delivering death or dying where they stood.

Even as the soldier expended one clip after another, drilled white-suited figures into bloody rags, littering the perimeter around the ZSU-23-4, they kept coming. One Spetsnaz wave after another was mowed down by the combined autofire from Bolan and Ulyatin. If nothing else, the Russian agent's grim resolve and lethal skill in killing her own, signaled Bolan she might be in the same ballpark as he.

Maybe.

Across the glacier, on the move up an incline where he could find cover behind a jagged wall of rock, Bolan took in the action near the gunships. Slobovka had fallen, and his commandos on his right flank were being scythed down, human bowling pins. Then another Hind became a fireball, and Thornton's air cavalry was reduced to countless shards and pieces of twisted scrap by the double-punch of

ZSU-23-4 cannon fire and the single Mi-24 blazing away with everything it had in its payload. Beyond the raging air war, winding down into abrupt death throes, someone had come up on Slobovka's blindside. But that someone was lost to Bolan's vision when the flaming shells of warbirds hammered to the glacier, erupting walls of fire and snow.

The suicide charge of the enemy succeeded in obliterating the antiaircraft cannon. Even as Bolan cut them down, they pitched enough grenades in and around the ZSU to wipe it off the face of the glacier in a series of blinding explosions, useless junk.

Then it happened.

The eruption along the west edge of the glacier even caused Bolan a second of fear-edged disbelief. He was close enough to the edge to worry about tumbling down into the gorge as the whole side of the glacier was sheared off. The soldier's only thought was to secure some point of higher ground, east. The only advantage he found was that the volcanic upheaval of snow, ice and rock most likely paralyzed each and every combatant.

For eternal stunned moments, clambering his way east up the high ground overlooking the glacier, the wall of snow, geysering into the air and out over both the gorge and glacier, shrouded everything in a blinding white haze that was cut only by winking saffron balls of fire. The seismic force, though, knocked Bolan off his feet. Nose-diving to the snow, his ears ringing, Bolan came up, searching the misty curtain. For damn sure, anything down in the gorge was buried alive.

But that had been Ivan the Terrible's intent all along. Foe or friendly, it didn't matter.

The Executioner gave his flank a quick search but found no sign of Ulyatin.

The SVR agent became the least of the soldier's worries in the next instant.

No sooner was the sky falling over the glacier than Bolan was forced to put her out of his mind as shadows burst from the raining white mist, pencil-tip flames of AK-47s stabbing the thin white blanket of cover.

It was do-or-die time.

9

Once again the world around Major Thornton felt ripped apart. His senses reeling, it all came rushing back to him in an eerie sense of déjà vu. First he had made his way up the east edge with a sort of numb determination to either kill or be killed.

Then he had found them on the LZ, surging from the choppers, weapons blazing at two figures on the far north edge of the glacier, and cut down what he could of the enemy. Then the Apache and the HueyCobras had streaked in, nearly colliding with the Hinds in their determination to take out the enemy warbirds. It had been a savage but beautiful sight, warbirds, flaming away, nose-to-nose. But it had been a lost cause from the onset, he feared, even if his flyboys had downed two more Hinds.

Now, the brief air war seemed like another eternity ago. The tumbling fireball, the sizzling streams of lead reaching out for him, had driven him to ground, kept him down, clinging to shadowy consciousness. Then he'd blacked out.

Once again he wondered how long he'd been out as his eyelids cracked open, sticky with blood.

Looking up through a shattered haze, hearing once more that fearsome roar of a series of tremendous explosions, the earth moving beneath his prone body, he summoned up whatever strength was left. He was scrabbling to haul in the M-16 when they came surging out of the white haze, tall, grim-faced shadows, faces so hard, eyes so dead that for a moment he didn't think they were human.

But they were, and he recognized the narrow-eyed, sloping face of his prime target.

Thornton couldn't suppress a strange chuckle that rumbled from somewhere deep in the angry churning of his belly. He looked up at Ivan the Terrible and said, "You want my name, rank and serial number, mister?"

Slobovka aimed his AK-47 at Thornton's face. "No. I want insurance. And as long as you cooperate, you will live. Have you ever been to Russia?"

"Kiss my ass, Ivan."

"Unlikely. However, I will see you kiss mine."

Before he could make that one last desperate grab for his M-16 and start spraying the bastards before they cut him down, Thornton felt himself hauled off the ground. Bloodied and bruised, he told himself he wasn't beaten. Not yet. As long as they let him breathe, there was a chance, as slim as it was.

In the corner of his eye, he glimpsed somebody taking one heavy toll of Spetsnaz casualties across the glacier. Whoever was kicking all that Russian ass, he wanted to pin a medal on that guy, even if it was the last thing he ever did.

GOING OUT QUIETLY had never been his style. Going out hard by dirty tricks inflicted on him by those supposed to be on his side wasn't something that sat well with Langston, either. In short, as he led seven of his mercs over the southern edge of the glacier, he had a damn good mind to settle up with Ivan the Terrible right then and there.

But he couldn't.

First, there was too much left to do, too much money to rake in, selling his services to the Council as he led the storm about to sweep preselected bodies of government. Second, Slobovka had sent to their deaths more than a few of his own men who couldn't scale the mountain fast enough. Obviously any soldier who wasn't quick enough, strong enough or mean enough wasn't good enough to be in the game to begin with. Casualties were to be expected—it was simply the cost of doing business. What was left of the Spetsnaz force in the gorge was now linked up with Langston, trailing him over the rise. Even with goggles over everyone's eyes to ward off the sun glaring off the snow, Langston couldn't find any happy faces. In fact, everyone looked good and pissed off to him, killing mean.

Last, but certainly not least, he'd received word yesterday through his eyes and ears in the organization that the big shots had set up shop just inside the Russian border—their destination, once they put India behind.

Even still, Langston was furious that Slobovka had brought the mountain down on them. He'd lost at least another five men, but he had to admit the opposition in the gorge had inflicted most of those casualties. Not to mention an obvious Sikh problem, by way of defection, had arisen. When the mountain came roaring down, what Sikhs were left standing had opted to bolt, run like hell and not look back. Langston had had a good mind back in the gorge to start cutting those yellow traitors down, but he couldn't afford to waste the ammunition. It didn't matter anyway. India would soon be history. The Sikhs had served their purpose, in a way. At worst, Langston had proved to the Council that he and Slobovka could go into a country, put together a militant group of malcontents and ship them off to parts unknown, take down a target, return them safely for future missions.

There was no time to mourn the dead, hate the AWOL Sikhs. Something was happening all over the glacier, and none of it looked good.

First, there was gunship wreckage all around the perimeter of Slobovka's transport choppers. Second, there was a gunman ripping away from the northern edge, covered by a jagged precipice dotted with boulders. The guy, one guy, was darting between the boulders, mowing down Spetsnaz commandos in some of the best free-fire killing Langston had seen in some time. It looked like the guy in white suit and goggles was firing steady and deadly with an Uzi submachine gun. In the other fist, a hand cannon was thundering away. It was double-fisted slaughter, the likes of which Langston knew only the most lethally skilled of professionals could pull off. Hell, bodies were piling up so fast, he figured a conveyor belt would be needed to haul off all the dead.

But the dead weren't going anywhere. It was clear

the Spetsnaz commandos had the single-minded goal to knock out the ZSU-23-4, keep that ballsy fighter from manning the antiaircraft cannon and blowing all of them clear back to New Delhi. Objective achieved, the surviving Spetsnaz fighters were charging the double-fisted dealer of death, but to no avail.

Slobovka had a prisoner, Langston saw. Major Thornton was flanked by two Spetsnaz commandos, with the GRU major holding the muzzle of an AK-47 at the base of the old warrior's skull.

Joining the GRU major, his mercs surrounding him, Langston locked a moment's stare with Thornton.

"You bastard," Thornton rasped. "Not a shred of honor in you."

"You picked the losing side, Major," Langston told the Special Forces soldier. "What can I say? Things happen. It isn't about honor anyway, Major. It's about changing with the times. The world loves itself. Hard and cold but true. Spare me the Stars and Stripes."

"Glad you could make it, Comrade Langston," Slobovka said, nearly yelling to be heard above the rotor wash and the ceaseless rattle and thunder of weapons fire.

"Damn near didn't make it, Major," Langston growled. "You want to explain why you felt it necessary to almost make me a sacrificial lamb?"

"You were warned," Slobovka growled. "If you want an apology, forget it. There is no time. We must evacuate."

"We'll talk later."

"You!" Slobovka roared across the glacier. "I have an American hostage. You will cease firing. Now! Or I will kill him!"

Langston watched as the lone warrior dropped the last trio of commandos, then his guns went silent. Langston was braced for the worst. Could be the guy had a rocket launcher and decided to go for broke. And there they stood, packed and neatly lined up.

Langston felt a sudden urge to be off the glacier. Dying at the hands of one lone, faceless enemy wasn't the way he wanted to go. Not now. Not when he was about to be the spearhead for a New World Order. Not to mention one of the richest mercenaries in the history of warfare.

This was not a good day to die.

THEY POPPED UP in the narrowed vision of his goggles, rushing like madmen up the rise, all rage and sizzling lead. The Executioner dropped them where they stood.

Sliding between the tight spaces of boulders, Bolan triggered the Uzi, sweeping them down while the .44 Magnum Desert Eagle managed some gruesome decapitating work. Crimson and pink was showering through the fine snow still falling from the massive explosion. After the first four, Bolan lost count, but figured he had toppled at least a dozen commandos by the time he heard the voice roaring for him to stop firing. Three more adversaries came at him, lunging over their own dead, and the Uzi in Bolan's fist stitched a neat crimson line across three chests.

Black smoke, mangled bodies and bloody snow

stretched away from the Executioner as he found another point of concealment behind a boulder. Cracking a fresh magazine into his Uzi, he surveyed his perimeter. Nothing was moving in on him at the moment, nothing but twitching limbs around the twisted scrap of the ZSU. A hideously wounded Spetsnaz commando wobbled to his feet, swinging up his AK-47. A 3-round burst from Bolan's Uzi sent that Russian into oblivion, silenced the awful wheezing from the enemy's mouth that betrayed a punctured lung.

For long moments, the echoes of the killing shot trailed over the glacier. Bolan took in the hostage situation near the transport ships. A force of thirty-plus had joined Slobovka. And where was Ulyatin?

A hard sweep of his left flank, and Bolan found no sign of the agent.

He listened as angry words lashed the icy air.

"Tell him your name!" Slobovka shouted.

A pause, then a grim chuckle from Slobovka's hostage.

"I'm Major Thornton, United States Special Forces. Whoever the hell you are over there, I order you to attack and blow these bastards clear off this mountain."

Bolan gave the major high marks for guts, but it was apparent that wasn't the response Slobovka wanted. Ivan the Terrible clipped Thornton over the head with the butt of his assault rifle, driving the major to his knees.

It was reaching another stage of critical mass. Bolan had a standoff. Evacuation was the objective of the enemy. If he let them off the mountain, he might lose them for good. There was no telling if Shiva's own HueyCobras were still in the fight, would even be up for pursuit, whether they were running low on fuel, ammo or nerve.

When another Hind swept in over the gorge, Bolan feared the worst for the operative's flyboys. The Hind hovered at a point east of the strong force. No doubt that top gun-crew was awaiting Slobovka's orders. The soldier sensed it all hinged on what he did or didn't do in the next few moments.

"We are leaving, whoever you are!" Slobovka called out. "Should you attempt to fire again, I will have no choice but to kill your Major Thornton. I know how much you Americans value the lives of your own. Should you prove me wrong, well, I will have no recourse but to also send my gunship to eliminate you."

Bolan gave that action a brief moment's thought. Why the GRU major didn't send the Hind barreling for his position right then told the Executioner either Slobovka's remaining gunship was out of ammo, or he was intent on conserving what firepower the war-bird had left.

Then Bolan discovered that Ulyatin was alive and well. From some point near the jagged western edge of the glacier, Bolan saw the woman expose her head, heard her yell, "Slobovka. You are finished. Even if you escape back into Russia, I will hunt you down like a dog and kill you by my own hand."

There was a long moment of tight silence, then Slobovka erupted with laughter.

"You dare laugh at me, you bastard!" Ulyatin raged, and Bolan feared she would just cut loose, raising her M-16, drawing a bead on the GRU major.

"Why, Lana Ulyatin. What a surprise. So, it is you that Department X sent to claim my head. You foolish woman. Whoever your friend is, there is no way, as you can plainly see, that I will not succeed. It would be far easier for you should you just come out and let me put a bullet through your brain. Yes. Like father, like daughter."

The revelation struck Bolan like a fist in the gut. More ugly truth had come to light. The woman's duty was vengeance, pure and simple. How many other lies had he been slapped with? Bolan wondered.

The Executioner decided the only thing that mattered was surviving the standoff. If Slobovka fled, then he'd chase the GRU major and his Spetsnaz killers clear to Moscow to get his own righteous pound of flesh.

ADJAN WAS LEADING what was left of his Sikh warriors out of the gorge. He was burning with rage and spotted the same light of fury in the eyes of Maraka and the others as they trudged and stumbled their way clear of the mouth, toward the tent. It was eerily quiet all around them, but the sounds of the avalanche and the screams of his dying Sikh brothers still rang in his ears.

The question now was how to proceed. There was no doubt about what they had to do in Adjan's mind, but he could read the skepticism and fear in the eyes of his brothers.

Checking his force, Adjan found they were down to less than twenty fighters. Somehow the word that Slobovka was going to blow the glacier had reached him last. Entrenched on the floor of the gorge, he had heard the call to pull back over the radio. The Russians and the Americans had grabbed precious minutes to retreat, then started hauling themselves up the gorge before Adjan and his men had time to assess their own casualties. It was insane, the two gunships, coming out of nowhere, stitching lines of death down the gorge, chopping up his own men and the front-line troops. Had Slobovka known something all along that he had kept only to himself and his own Spetsnaz commandos?

It didn't matter. As far as Adjan was concerned, he was finished with the Russians. The only way he would ever see an independent Sikh state of Khalistan would be by his own hand. Already he was planning attacks in the streets of major Indian cities: car bombs, assassinations, planting explosives in Hindu shrines all over the country. He still had plenty of firepower, plenty of plastique to spare, but it was all back in the village.

Adjan found the slaughter inside the tent. He wasn't shocked by the sight of all the dead who had obviously died horrible and violent deaths. Rather, he grew self-confident that he'd made the right decision to abandon Slobovka.

"What do we do now?"

Adjan slowly turned and looked Maraka dead in the eye. "Now? We return home."

"To do what?"

"To carry on our fight."

"Without the Russians?"

Adjan gritted his teeth. "We do not need the Russians. The Russians used us, discarded us like so much garbage. It is pure luck we were not crushed when the good Major Slobovka decided to bring the mountain down on us." Adjan ran a cold eye over his warriors. "The village, our people throughout the Punjab, are with us to death. Are we warriors who stand strong and hold our ground to the bitter end, or do we say it is no use and cringe in the dark like old women or dogs who grovel when they are kicked?"

Fire lit their eyes, Adjan saw. They were inspired. They would carry on the war, go down to the last man until the Indian government capitulated and gave them what they wanted. No man, he knew, wanted to be shrouded with the stench of cowardice.

"We are with you, Adjan, until death," Maraka said in an unwavering voice of cold determination.

Adjan looked at the sprawled bodies and spit. "Let us get out of here. Should the Russians come back for us, they will end up like this."

He swept out of the tent, fueled with righteous rage. It was far from being over. In fact, he determined, the war against India had only just begun.

Who was going to stop them?

10

It was a fiasco of the worst kind, but were they defeated? McNeary couldn't believe what he saw when his vision began to clear. They came down the ledge, only six of his commandos left. They trudged or limped, white suits torn and bloody.

For a moment, the near crushing death experience swirled with the full weight of its horror through his mind. McNeary had clung to the ledge during the avalanche for dear life, his senses shattered by the roar of free-falling snow and ice. Luckily he had cleared most of the thundering force, found shelter beneath the jagged lip of a precipice. But something, ice or snow, whatever, had slammed off his skull, hammering him into a nauseous sea of utter blackness.

McNeary checked his troops. Barber, his second-in-command, was bleeding like a stuck pig from a deep gash across his forehead.

Barber vented his agony and rage. "I want those Russian bastards, and Langston. I don't give a damn what it takes, but I want to see them dead by my own hand."

No doubt, it had turned personal.

Suddenly McNeary heard the faint sound of rotors,

growing from the south. The CIA strike force instantly hugged the wall, weapons poised as the insectlike bleat of chopper blades knifed up the gorge.

Waiting, McNeary gave the bed of death below a quick but hard search. A few arms and legs and the muzzle of a rifle poked out of the snow. It was useless to search for any more survivors.

Braced to launch a 40 mm grenade from his M-203, McNeary saw the shadowy bulk of the metallic dragonfly surge through the mist—a Huey-Cobra. It was one of theirs, but *only* one. Moments later, the gunship lowered, hovered near the ledge. Racked by pain, McNeary still managed the four-foot drop into the fuselage, snow pluming around the open doorway from the rotor wash. One by one, the troops hopped in, but McNeary went straight for the cockpit.

"Status report?" the specialist leader asked the pilot, McGruder.

The helmeted pilot swiveled his head. "The word is grim, sir. We downed one of the Hinds, but I'm afraid one of theirs got Cowler and Thompkins. The one Hind must've been called back. It veered off. No pursuit on our part, sir, we're low on fuel, down to one Hellfire. What the hell happened here, sir?"

"Goddamn Ivan brought the mountain down on us, that's what the hell happened."

"The others, sir?"

"History. Buried alive."

The pilot cursed. "Two things, sir. One—a quick surveillance of the glacier from the south, and it looks like they've got a standoff situation. The enemy is set to fly. It also looks like we've got two of our own on the northern edge. Would appear our side did some serious damage to Ivan.''

Pollock and Ulyatin, McNeary knew, and felt a surge of hope stir some fire in his belly.

"The other thing?"

"Coming up the gorge from the south," the pilot answered, "I counted maybe twenty turbans, moving hard, due south."

The Sikhs. Defecting. But why?

"Could've chopped them up into human cheese, sir, but like I said, we couldn't spare the ammo. Where to, sir?"

"Let's go round up Pollock."

"That's one lucky SOB, that Pollock," Barber snarled.

McNeary felt a grim smile cut his lips. Didn't he know it, he thought. From there on, McNeary decided to latch on to the colonel's coattails. After all, it sure looked like the man knew how to ride the thunder, kick some serious ass. He wouldn't tell his men, of course, but as far as he was concerned, Pollock was in charge.

THEY WERE GOING TO FLY, and there wasn't a thing Bolan could do to stop their evacuation. Even if he had the available rocket firepower to blow them off the LZ, the soldier knew he couldn't do that. After all, the enemy had Major Thornton, and the man had proved his commitment to duty and honor.

The evidence of Thornton's integrity and courage was strewed all over the glacier.

Slowly Bolan marched down the incline for the level stretch of the icefield. The last of the Spetsnaz force and who he believed were the CIA traitors boarded the gunships. Bolan figured Slobovka was down to thirty guns. They'd cut the numbers, but it wasn't enough, nor was it over.

The enemy gunships lifted off and veered to the east, sailing off the glacier.

Moments earlier, the Executioner had sighted the Huey, south, then their warbird had vanished beyond the jagged teeth ringing the glacier in that direction.

Uzi low by his side, Bolan closed on Ulyatin. The two of them stood, alone, in hard silence for a good half minute. For several fleeting moments, the soldier sensed the agent softening her hard-as-nails veneer, seeming desperate to say something.

She broke Bolan's penetrating stare, her gaze wandering over the slaughter zone. The angry licking of hungry flames and the stench of blood and burning fuel pierced Bolan's senses as he waited for her to speak.

If nothing else, they were alive. But a slew of questions rolled through his mind. Was she really an SVR agent? What else might she know about Slobovka or his plans that she might be keeping to herself?

Bolan took in the hellzone. In all directions, death stretched away from them. It had been a brief but furious fight, and it had left him with a sour taste in his mouth. Slobovka was gone, and Thornton was a prisoner of Ivan the Terrible. Insurance, right, the GRU major had said.

Well, the Executioner was intent on making his own claim on that insurance.

Finally Ulyatin spoke. "Now you know."

"Slobovka murdered your father, that's all I know. Is your mission official or unofficial, Agent Ulyatin?"

"Both. I am exactly who I told you I was." She clenched her jaw, and Bolan read the all too familiar fires of vengeance in her eyes. "My father was a top-ranking KGB agent in charge of subversion and sabotage during the early stages of the Afghanistan war. However, after a year of witnessing the bloody fighting and brutality, he came to realize that our country would become mired in something like your Vietnam War. We underestimated the strength and determination of the Afghan guerrillas. When Spetsnaz moved in, under Major Slobovka's iron hand, they began systematically eradicating entire villages—genocide, by fire, by aerial bombardment, even by chemical warfare. They even took to booby-trapping children's toys. My father saw a prolonged war of atrocity such as this would not benefit Russia. He made the mistake of filing an official report with the KGB, objecting to the indiscriminate slaughter tactics of Slobovka."

Bolan filled in the blanks when she paused. "So, Slobovka killed him."

"In cold blood. He called a meeting that was allegedly to discuss new operations. Slobovka walked right up behind my father and shot him in the back of the head. Now, I hope you understand my thirst to kill Slobovka personally."

"That doesn't change the fact he's most likely going to disappear inside the Russian border to do whatever it is he's going to do."

"Nothing has changed. In fact, it will only serve to make our mission that much easier. He cannot hide from contacts inside Russia."

Before Bolan could ask for details, the Huey roared up over the glacier. From its point of ascent, Bolan assumed the flyboys had been searching for survivors.

When the Huey touched down near Bolan, the soldier discovered Shiva and a skeleton hardforce was all that had escaped the fury of the avalanche.

Disembarking, Shiva gave the carnage a grim eyeballing. He whistled softly, as if admiring the slaughter.

There was an apologetic tone in Shiva's voice as he told Bolan, "My people were right, Colonel—you and Agent Ulyatin gave them a serious headache."

Bolan felt an urgent need to be in the air, en route for Slobovka's next destination. There was an edge in his voice. "We can't take all the credit. Slobovka snatched Major Thornton. If Thornton hadn't hit their blindside, things might have turned out a little different for us."

"You know they'll kill Thornton, don't you?" Shiva stated.

"All I know is the man was alive last time I saw him. What I know is that I damn sure want him on our side."

"All right, Colonel, here it is. I fucked up in the gorge. Cost me most of my people. But I've got a contingency plan and a backup team on standby. How do you feel about us flying straight into Russia to nail these bastards?''

"I don't see we have any choice."

"Right. We lost a battle but not the war." Shiva seemed unable to resist giving the hellgrounds one last surveillance. "You did all right, Colonel. You, too, Agent Ulyatin."

"Save the congratulations," Bolan said. "We haven't won a damn thing. How long before we can get airborne for Russia?"

"Soon as we get back to the command post in our Sikh village. I can put in the call from there." Shiva paused, then said, "Oh, one other item."

Bolan froze in midstride for the gunship. He looked back at Shiva, not liking the man's tone of voice.

"My pilots spotted what was left of the Sikhs beating a hasty exit south. My feeling is they're cutting out on their Russian backers. Makes our job a little easier."

The news changed Bolan's immediate plan. Should they fly out of India now, the soldier knew he stood to lose his one real chance to take care of the grim business regarding the Sikh butchers. A week, days at the most, and the Sikhs could well disappear, without a trace, into Pakistan or Afghanistan, never to be seen or heard from again, never having to account for their atrocities.

"Doesn't make anything easier," Bolan told Shiva. "It just alters our timetable a little."

"How come I get the feeling you're about to tell

me, Colonel, you've still got unfinished business in this country?''

''Because I do. With or without you. We'll fly and talk.''

Blood racing to pick up the scent of the hunt, Bolan hopped into the gunship.

Unfinished business, right.

Killing business.

IT HADN'T BEEN a good day for Judd Langston. Forget the fact his force had nearly been wiped out by both enemy fire and friendly treachery. Never mind that the Sikhs had bailed out at the first sign of trouble.

No, what concerned Langston was seeing the other half of the ten million, promised by the Council, to be deposited in his Hong Kong account. Now he was faced with a potential major setback. Undoubtedly it wouldn't look good when they landed at the Russian base. If his source was right, the organization would be there, waiting. First order of business would be the men assessing the damage in India, maybe scrambling to keep the fallout from raining down on their heads. The worst-case scenario would be abandoning the project altogether, but Langston didn't think they'd do that. Sure, the Indian government would be up in arms, demanding answers, furious with themselves for letting the Americans call the shots on their turf. So the Indians would be looking for scapegoats, presumably, he hoped, combing the Punjab for suitable Sikh prey.

So India was a wash, but it had always been simply a springboard for bigger things. Time to move on.

The only plus was the GRU major's trucks with plows had cleared the snow off a strip of the plain. Now they were airborne, a good hour in the sky, flying northwest over the Himalayas.

Puffing on a cigarette, standing in the aft of the Antonov, the throaty rumble of the big bird's turbo-prop engines in his ears, Langston gave his survivors a long hard look. Out of nowhere, he felt that all-too-familiar ball of ice lodge in his belly, felt his gaze narrow to mere slits, knew his eyes were glinting with murder, as the idea took shape in his mind. And these men had fought and killed beside him long enough to know the ''look.''

Langston weighed the odds. Thirty-five Russians, including Slobovka and the flight crew. One word, and Langston knew the eight of them could turn their M-16s on Ivan, cut them down, hijack the Antonov. Later they'd toss the bodies out and tell the Council that Slobovka and his commandos had simply been casualties of war.

Peebles, his slate gray eyes shining from the shadows of the soft yellow overhead spilling over his heavily bristled face, said, ''I can fly this thing.''

True. Both Peebles and Farmer, Langston knew, had piloted AC-130 gunships for the CIA during the Vietnam War, logged more than ample hours while churning up the jungles of Southeast Asia with death from above. Langston figured the specs of the Antonov couldn't be too different from a Spectre's.

''You want to do it?'' Farmer said.

Langston debated the problem. Returning with just his team would look suspicious. Given his track record, the Council would smell something, possibly cancel his contract. Tack on the fact that the Sikhs had gone AWOL and that they might have a faceless opposition chasing them into Russia, well, there was still that five million to collect. He could always settle up with Slobovka later.

"No. We ride it out," Langston said.

Langston discovered he had made the call not a moment too soon. Out of the forward gloom, he found Slobovka rolling for him. Langston met the GRU major amidships.

"Everything under control, Major?"

"As well as can be expected, Mr. Langston, under the present circumstances. We have not been followed."

Langston glanced at Major Thornton, who was bound with rope, hand and foot, guarded in the forward section by Spetsnaz commandos. "What about him?"

"He will be interrogated, at my convenience. If he can provide no details about who might be after us, or when they might attempt to strike next, you know what will happen."

"He doesn't know anything," Langston said.

"Nor do you about exactly who attacked us. Perhaps he is holding information back, just as you kept secrets from him."

A slight or a warning? Langston wondered, then saw Slobovka run a narrow gaze of suspicion over his troops.

"I get the feeling I walked in on something. I trust you are not still annoyed about what I had to do back in the gorge, Mr. Langston."

"My only concern is seeing the project through to a successful end."

"And collecting your money, of course."

"I'm not in this for ideology, Major. Once we take down the Kremlin and your people are in place, I walk. And there's something else you should know. The Council has set up shop near our base."

Anger flashed through Slobovka's eyes. "This is the first I have heard of this."

"Well, you're hearing about it now. I would have told you earlier, when I was informed, but you had your hands full."

Slobovka seemed to ponder something. "It means they intend to accelerate the timetable."

"Could just mean they want to be close to the action."

Slobovka smiled. "Mr. Langston, we have succeeded so far in our mission, but the most difficult and dangerous task is just ahead. Regrettably we write the Sikhs off as hard-learned experience. However, there will be other countries where we can train and mobilize entire armies. In the future, we just need to exercise better judgment." There was a hard pause, then Slobovka added, "I do hope we can continue to work together as we have done so far."

A warning. Langston knew he'd have to watch his back from there on. He was in it for the money, whereas Ivan lied to himself that it was all about restoring the old Communist order. Conflicting desires and objectives meant neither of them could trust the other. Fine. Langston would keep his rage to himself, not forget the terror he had survived in the gorge.

Langston ground out his cigarette beneath his boot heel. "If you'll excuse me, Major, I'm going to catch some shut-eye before we land."

Even as he made his way back to his men, Langston felt Slobovka's piercing stare boring into the back of his head. When he took his seat, Langston found the GRU major turning on his heel, heading for his own men. Something then clutched Langston's gut with an unshakable chill. If he didn't miss his guess, Langston would have sworn he had just glimpsed the "look" on Ivan's face.

A bad day, he thought, might just turn downright awful. But Judd Langston wasn't going to suffer through any more fiascos and near misses. If Slobovka didn't lose the "look," and quick, he would have to give the order. A man had to learn how to adjust to unforeseen circumstances, after all.

THE EXECUTIONER SENSED Shiva was waiting for him to make the call.

They were gathered in the command post, back at the Sikh hut. No sooner had they touched down than Shiva was on the radio. But he had contacted the backup team at the air base south of Delhi rather than call them in. It was Bolan who had ordered the delay.

During the ninety-minute flight from the gorge, the soldier had made it clear he was going after the Sikh force, no matter what. Unfortunately there had been no sighting of the Sikh defectors. But with all the hills, valleys, gorges and rhododendron forests that broke up an uneven, snow-drenched wasteland leading away from the Himalayan foothills, it would be difficult, if not impossible, to sight the Sikhs from the air. And with the HueyCobra low on fuel, a thorough aerial recon had been out of the question. Along the way, Bolan had spotted numerous villages, large and small, dotting the rugged landscape.

Now Bolan was seated across the large wooden table, fixing Shiva, then Ulyatin with a steady gaze. Behind the Executioner, Shiva's six men were stripping and cleaning their weapons, their silence grim but edged with mounting impatience. In one corner of the large room, crackling flames from a cast-iron stove were consuming the three dozen satellite photos of the Russian base north of the Afghanistan border.

They were waiting for an answer.

There was no decision to make as far as Bolan was concerned. The Huey was fueled, ready to fly.

The Executioner then let his stare wander over the trio of turbaned Sikhs who were Shiva's informants. According to Shiva, those men knew exactly where Mokhan Adjan and Bant Maraka were holed up. Better still, the Sikh eyes-and-ears had also informed Bolan directly it was Adjan and Maraka who had committed the slaughter on I-66.

Prime target established, the only thing left to do in the immediate present was to establish contact with Adjan and Maraka, then terminate with extreme prejudice.

Shiva cleared his throat. He appeared nervous and agitated to Bolan. "Up to now, Colonel, both myself and Ulyatin have worked this with you on a need-to-know basis. Pretty much only because we needed to see how the numbers fell."

"What's changed to make you decide to let me in?"

"Fate. Call it a battlefield decision. I've known about Agent Ulyatin's vendetta against Slobovka all along. I don't care who gets him, as long as the man goes down. Beyond that, well, you've seen the photos. I believe that the power structure of this conspiracy is at that compound. We're looking at a large paramilitary installation, complete with antiaircraft batteries, armored vehicles, barracks, satellite dishes. Could be as many as two, three hundred Spetsnaz commandos bunkered there, but I don't think so. My sources inform me Slobovka's army is sizable but doesn't surpass two hundred guns."

"The problem we face," Ulyatin said, "is how many and who is involved beyond the compound."

"The problem we face," Bolan said grimly, "is destroying the compound and living to root out any conspirators."

"We discussed the strategy, Colonel," Shiva said, "and we both agreed. No other way than to go in hard. Parachute in, four teams, moving in on the compound, north, south, east and west. Luckily the weather in this part of Russia isn't nearly as bad as it is farther north. From my reports, I gather that most of Russia is enduring one of the worst winters on record since 1941."

"The weather makes a problem for both us and them," Bolan countered. "We deal with it."

"Right," Shiva agreed. "But I can keep that AC-130 up in the air only so long. That's provided, of course, it isn't picked up by radar and a few MiGs don't blow it out of the sky. It's all dicey, at best."

"No choice," Bolan said. "We go with what we have. The backup team, the Spectre and who's in this room."

"Then we're clear on this," Shiva said.

"Crystal," Bolan answered.

"We've got ninety minutes inside the compound before the gunship drops the sky on the place, even if our heads are in the way."

"Make the call on the spot," Bolan said. "I'm not going in this with a death wish. We're getting a little ahead of ourselves."

Bolan fell into hard silence. He looked pointedly at the Sikhs, then locked Shiva's stare. The soldier had already told the agent he was going after the Sikh terrorists, with or without him. All the Executioner wanted was for the Huey to drop him off near the terrorist haven, confirmed by Shiva's informants to be in a large village, one hundred miles northeast. Bolan decided it was time to put a moment of truth on Shiva. It wasn't a question of priorities; rather, the soldier wanted a clean sweep, eliminate one group of savages before committing himself to the next hellground.

"Well?" Bolan said.

"Understand something, Colonel. What happened this morning is going to reach the Indian government, then the Indian military steps in. There'll be enough flak flying to grind all of us into pulp, meaning we need to put this country behind us ASAP. If I don't reestablish contact with the commander of the backup force in two hours, the mission is aborted, and that's straight from my people. Without myself or Agent Ulyatin, you don't get into Russia. Unless, of course, you hike it over the Himalayas and through Afghanistan.''

"You in or out?" the Executioner asked coldly.

Shiva cut a mean grin. "I was going to say, be all that as it may, I'm with you. Let's just call it team spirit."

It was the only thing Bolan wanted to hear right then. Uzi slung over his shoulder, the soldier was out of his chair, eager to settle up with the targeted Sikh butchers of innocents.

11

Adjan wasn't pleased with their reception on his second homecoming. At first, he became indignant, then grew angry. Finally deep suspicion settled in.

Sensing something wrong, Adjan ordered Maraka to stop the truck, a vehicle they had received as a gift from a brother Sikh revolutionary, north of his home village of Abutani. His AK-47 slung across his shoulder, Adjan hopped out of the cab. With growing disbelief, he turned, watching as his men disembarked from the truck. Down to a mere eighteen warriors, they leaped out of the bed or jumped down from the sides, where they had clung to the wooden slats during the dangerous two-hour journey over open and potentially hostile territory.

Finally, as his force gathered around him, Adjan fixed a grim gaze on the dome of the temple in the distance. With heavy legs, he began leading his warriors down the main congested street. Right away he read the fear in the eyes of the villagers, then he spotted contempt in the eyes of the older men. This was insanity! This was the village of his birthplace, and he was being shunned and shirked, as if he were a leper. What had happened here? On their previous triumphant return from America, the villagers had heaped gifts and adulation on them, the whole village infected by a feverish desire for their own independent Khalistan.

Now this madness. Adjan thought he might as well have been back in America. He felt completely alone, lost, adrift.

Unwelcome.

No matter, he told himself, marching on, squaring his shoulders, knocking aside an old man who had unwittingly crossed his path. The temple was still under his control. A sizable arms cache was hidden in the cellar. A large chest, concealed in a locked trapdoor, was stuffed with rubles, rupees and Yankee dollars, almost a half million American. And Ranbar Mohalla and ten loyal followers had pledged to guard the temple to death.

"Why do they look at us as if we are criminals?" Maraka snarled.

Why, indeed? But Maraka's angry words fell on deaf ears, sounded to Adjan as if they came from miles away. Suddenly he was tumbling into the past. Shrouded in the misty veil of yesteryear, Adjan hoped that, by recalling the past, he would find renewed strength to deal with the trials of the present.

The temple's dome loomed, majestic and glistening in the afternoon sun, in Adjan's rage-focused vision. It beckoned, called him forward. He found himself so hypnotized by the dome, he wasn't even aware of the snow, melting under the sun's glare, turning to slush then mud with each forward step.

No, the dome of the Abutani temple was not made of gold such as the dome of the Golden Temple at

Amritsar. But the dome was still the same symbolic representation of an inverted lotus flower. By pointing back toward the earth, the inverted lotus flower was a symbol of the Sikhs' concern with matters of the world. Indeed, Adjan's older brother and sister had died for that symbol, cut down in the slaughter at the Golden Temple by the bullets of Indian soldiers, more than a decade earlier. Like the fiercely independent blood of his family, Adjan had never believed in falling into the same trap that ensnared so many Sikhs. Instead of going to the universities in Delhi, Bombay, Calcutta, slipping quietly into place in the Hindu-dominated Indian society as a mechanic or engineer, doctor or lawyer, Adjan always believed he was destined for something far greater, far more noble than the seeking of, then the clinging to the creature comforts and pleasures of the world.

Adjan was a warrior with vision.

But doubt was now creeping into his resolve. Was it all a hopeless fight? Why was he suddenly so stricken with great sorrow? Why did he feel such overwhelming fury that he wanted to turn his AK-47 on his own people, slaughter them where they stood? Didn't they see his fight was their fight? Didn't they know they would never be recognized as a great and proud and worthy people, never free or in control of their own lives as long as the Hindus monopolized the power in India?

Then, out of nowhere, the words of a great guru rang with haunting clarity through his mind. "None of us ever receive what we truly need, much less what we want. The sorrow of the world is created in direct proportion to the extent of man's own selfish desires. Whether it is the pursuit of money or power, recognition of oneself by his peers or the sating of the lust for flesh, it is all the same. Take caution, young Mokhan Singh Adjan. I look into your eyes, and I fear I see a young man who is set to embark on a perilous journey that can only end in death and destruction. Remember, all one has of true value is what is in one's heart. The Universe does not care what you have—rather, It wants what you are. Just because we, as Sikhs, are concerned with the world, it does not mean we must be consumed by the world. It is why our surname is 'Lion.' ' "

Exactly what did the old guru mean? Adjan wondered. Was he a fool? How could a man, any man, be truly free, when the world's own selfish desires meant to crush him? No, to turn the other cheek was cowardice. If a man believed in his own words, believed in himself, then he had to stand alone, take action. Fight back.

Adjan was jolted back to the moment when he saw the short, stocky Mohalla stride through the gate. The worry etched all over Mohalla's craggy features didn't bolster Adjan with confidence.

"There is trouble, I am afraid," Mohalla told Adjan. "How shall I say, bad news travels fast. I am told the criminal Hindu government is mobilizing an army to invade the Punjab."

So there it was, Adjan thought, war. The thunder, then the screech of a train pulling into the depot at the east edge of Abutani jarred Adjan. It would be too risky to reach Amritsar by train, then travel on foot across the border into Pakistan. Evacuation of Abutani, then flight from the country was the only logical course of action. But Adjan was eager for a fight with the Indian soldiers.

"What do we do now?" Adjan heard Maraka ask.

"We will hold the temple the rest of the day," Adjan told the group. "If the soldiers come for us, then we fight. If not, well, by nightfall it will be safer to travel by vehicle to the Pakistan border. We have sympathetic comrades there who will provide us refuge. It has obviously become too hot in India for us to remain here. Six months, a year at the worst, we wait in Pakistan. Then we return with a large fighting force. I will spit on the cowards you see in our village when we force the government to give us Sikhs our own sovereign nation. When we return, this country will tremble before us."

"What happened with the Russians?" Mohalla asked.

Adjan scowled. "I will tell you inside the temple. Let me just say, we do not need the Russians, we do not need anybody who is not one of us."

Adjan read the fire in their eyes, knew right then, beyond any doubt, they would fight by his side to the death. With long strides, he led what was left of his warriors across the courtyard. There were preparations to make. At least the money and the weapons were safe.

It struck him right then, recalling the old guru's words, exactly what his life, his destiny, was all about—pride, living as a warrior, and pride, dying like a man, if he had to.

He was Sikh, after all. He was Lion.

THERE WOULD BE nothing fancy, nothing tricky about the hit on the temple. Strike fast, hard and last. Hit, take them down, move on. It was as basic as it could get.

The problem Bolan faced was lack of concrete intel on the numbers. Daylight also erased the advantage of stealth.

As the Huey touched down at the eastern edge of the large village of Abutani, Bolan hit the ground, running, leading his team at a hard jaunt down the main dirt street. He had three minutes and counting to get to the front wall, cover the twenty-yard stretch of no-man's-land that was the courtyard, blast his way through the front door. The Huey was already en route, veering north. From there, the warbird would set down in the rear of the temple, unload Shiva and his six men. They would go in, guns blazing. If it was armed, it was dead. All in all, a classic pincer attack. If the enemy Sikhs were flushed for either exit, they were doomed.

Easier said than done, Bolan knew, closing hard on the front wall.

Uzi poised to fire, flanked by Ulyatin and the three Sikh informants, the soldier surged past the sea of gathering faces of suspicion, curiosity and fear. Senses alive for any sign of sudden movement, Bolan found none of the villagers armed or brazen enough to get in their way. At least not yet.

Bolan fixed combat tunnel vision on the temple's dome, looming with each swift step. From the air, he had managed a quick but hard look at the target site. It wasn't the Taj Mahal or the Golden Temple at Amritsar, but it was large enough to bunker a sizable, well-armed force.

The Sikh informants had filled in some of the blanks about the hardsite layout and numbers. At least a dozen armed followers of Adjan were entrenched in the temple, converting the building, weeks ago, from a place of worship and prayer into a fortress. And the hardsite was complete, they had told Bolan, with an arms cache, ranging in hardware from assault rifles to rocket launchers. There were two entrances, front and rear. Once through the front, it would be a different matter. A concentric retaining wall ran around the main prayer chamber, with entrances that branched off to other chambers. It was a one-story viper's nest, but there was a basement with a labyrinth of tunnels. Bolan meant to cut them off before they slithered below. But gut instinct warned him the Sikhs would stand, fight and die where they stood. Ground zero, damn right.

It was also a long shot that Adjan and Maraka were even inside the temple, but Bolan had to roll the dice, hope for the best while grimly intent on delivering the worst. He was on Shiva's clock, after all. The CIA operative had radioed the backup team during the flight, selecting a suitable rice field, east of Abutani, that looked to be the only decent LZ for the Spectre.

After their defection at the hands of their Russian masters, the soldier had to believe the two main butchers of innocent Americans would return to base, gather in the reinforcements, beef up on firepower, then plot a course of flight for the border.

There was only one way to find out how it would go down.

Bolan crouched beside the opening of the front wall, one of the Sikhs right on his heels. Directly across from the soldier, Ulyatin took up position with the other two Sikhs. It was all planned, right down to the four fragmentation grenades in the pockets of Bolan's arctic white camou fatigues.

The soldier gave the stretch of no-man's-land leading to the arched main entrance a hard once-over. No movement.

Then the Executioner put one last, searching gaze on Ulyatin, then the Sikhs. It didn't escape him that the Sikhs could be marching him into a death trap.

One of the Sikhs, Singh Nanak, had to have read the Executioner's suspicious look. "We are with you against them. Trust us."

"I'm going to have to," the soldier replied.

Bolan broke from the cover of the wall, leading the dash across the courtyard, his gaze riveted on the main entrance. Then he caught the bleating of rotor blades, spotted the gunship swooping for the temple from the north a moment later.

Suddenly autofire was tracking him. A heartbeat before he secured cover behind the wall to the entrance, slugs gouging out stone above his head, Bolan caught sight of two turbaned figures with AK-47s emerge into the murk of the arched entrance. Obviously the enemy had been on full alert.

Time to turn on the heat.

Plucking a grenade and pulling the pin, Bolan nodded at Ulyatin.

"We will cover! Go!" Nanak roared.

Before Bolan knew what the Sikh was going to do, he saw Nanak break cover, hold his ground and unleash his AK-47 at the shadows in the entrance. Nanak's fellow Sikh warriors leaped into the open, cutting loose with the same reckless fury.

A line of crimson holes erupted up Nanak's torso, but the Sikh bellowed in rage, held down the trigger of his assault rifle. Nanak was toppling, absorbing the return barrage as Bolan and Ulyatin lobbed the armed bombs toward the pencil-tip flames stabbing the gloom.

Downrange twin saffron flashes ripped through the enemy. One final look at Nanak, knowing beyond any doubt the man was dead, and Bolan plunged into the smoke and cordite.

STILL STINGING from the Russian sucker punch back at the gorge, McNeary was savagely determined to pull this hit off with clean, lightning finality. In and out. No hesitation, no doubts, no snafus, no friendly casualties. By the numbers, as outlined by Pollock, cut down anything in a turban that moved and carried a weapon. He figured he owed a blood victory to the memory of the men he'd lost, to Pollock. But most of all, he owed himself some grim payback.

It didn't take but a moment for McNeary to get busy reclaiming some self-respect, inflicting some ugly damage, rekindling the fires of all his warrior skills earned in blood dues over two decades of doing the Company's dirty jobs in remote, little-known and even less cared about hellholes around the world.

No sooner was he leaping out of the gunship, spearheading the charge on the temple's rear than four pairs of wild eyes beneath wine-colored turbans popped up in his gun sights, gave him the perfect excuse to vent his rage. On the run, McNeary squeezed the M-16's trigger. The Sikh foursome spun, screamed as a din of autofire split the air around them. McNeary was fueled with surging adrenaline and searing confidence at the sight of his troops helping him chop through the enemy with relentless lethal precision.

Outstanding. Four down, but how many more were inside?

Blood and shredded cloth taking to the air in the doorway, raining on him, McNeary forged into the torchlit gloom of the narrow circular hallway. Coming in low, fanning the hall in both directions with his M-16, he led one three-man team to the north, while the other fighting trio shadowed south. According to Nanak, the retaining wall encircled the main prayer chamber. It was there he would find the bulk of the Sikh fanatics, armed to the teeth.

He did.

The rattle of weapons fire, a berserkerlike howl followed by two thunderclaps of frag grenades erupting deadly payloads sounded from the eastern side of the temple. That would be Pollock and his team, McNeary hoped, shoving death right in someone's face.

As he followed the cursing, shouting and the short

bursts of autofire, McNeary quickly reached an opening in the retaining wall. And found all hell had broken loose in the main prayer chamber.

At least twenty Sikhs were scrambling all over the place, firing at darting shadows at the eastern end of the room. It was only a fleeting glimpse, but McNeary spotted the tall silhouette he identified as Pollock. Even as Sikh bullets whined off the stone and marble around the man, Pollock moved from opening to opening, unleashing his Uzi. Then Pollock hurled a grenade into the room. The fireball's countless flying pieces of steel shrapnel added death and gruesome chaos to the enemy's frenzy.

When the Sikhs started to move his way, McNeary and his shock commandos ripped long, sweeping bursts through the prayer chamber, heaping scythed and gutted corpses to the marble floor, which became awash with slick crimson in a matter of seconds.

The Sikhs were pinned, cut off, hemmed in. It looked good until one of the Sikhs grabbed an RPG-7, wheeled and sent the warhead rocketing on a true line that seemed to come straight for McNeary's face. The CIA agent hit the floor behind the wall, felt the slipstream as the missile swept overhead. He fully expected to be blown clear through the dome, but the explosion rocked the air at some point, well to the rear. Looking back, McNeary peered into the boiling smoke, far down the narrow alcove adjacent to the hall.

Close.

Stoked with renewed fury, he was up and cracking a fresh clip into his M-16. As determined as he was,

McNeary found the Sikhs spraying autofire in all directions, obviously hell-bent on fighting and dying on the sacred ground of their temple.

McNeary obliged two of the Sikh terrorists, milking 3-round bursts, stitching 5.56 mm lead up their backsides.

The enemy came back at his position with tracking streams of autofire. Braving the lead screaming off stone and marble all around him, McNeary bolted down the hall, searching for another opening through which he could hit the enemy's flank. Even with the Sikh force shredded in two, he judged the roar of the hellstorm, heard the sudden lack of men screaming in agony and knew the raging battle was far from over. In fact, McNeary was sure it had only just begun.

Reaching another opening, he restrained himself from checking his watch. If they all died in the temple, it wouldn't matter a goat's ass if they made that LZ.

McNeary wheeled around the edge of the wall, firing his M-16 on full auto for all he was worth.

12

Even before the initial onslaught, Bolan knew it would be touch-and-go. One of the most dangerous moments came when the soldier led the surge through the arched entrance. Any law-enforcement officer wouldn't hesitate to lay down the hard facts of life about being the first one through the door. If the enemy was entrenched and hidden from immediate view, Bolan could be cut down before he knew what hit him.

Pumped on adrenaline, Bolan was inside and moving down the hallway when he heard the reinforcements arrive to seal the rear exit. It sounded as if Shiva and his commandos had come in, blazing away. So far, so good.

Just like the Sikhs had said, Bolan found himself in a circular hall, torchlit and cut with narrow alcoves and offshoots leading to other rooms on his flank. Passing the entrances, he found nothing moving. Not yet anyway.

Then the Executioner swept across a break in the wall, discovered the Sikh informants had proved to be trustworthy. The prayer chamber was a war room, complete with large tables heaped with assault rifles and rocket launchers, and a hardforce of twenty plus.

Bolan's Uzi went to work, finding targets right away. He was sprinting for the next break in the retaining wall when he heard the roar of combined autofire at the rear, glimpsed Ulyatin and their Sikh allies cranking the killing mode up a notch.

A darting shadow, Bolan moved from opening to opening before tracking enemy autofire could find him, shaving the hardforce by six guns.

Then several things happened in the next heartbeat, threatening to turn the tide against the Executioner and his force. As grimly expected, the Sikh fanatics fought with the same suicidal fever pitch the soldier had seen on the glacier when engaging Spetsnaz. A hornet's nest of lead was screaming all around him, certain to score his flesh if he didn't do something fast.

Then, as Bolan armed a frag bomb, five, maybe six turbaned shadows poured through those offshoots on Bolan's rear. Ulyatin and their Sikh allies were locked in a sudden death struggle, weapons from all combatants flaming away at one another at point-blank range.

A swift underhand pitch, and Bolan sent the steel egg bouncing right into the middle of the war room. There, Sikhs were scrambling, some toppling from the searching autofire from Shiva and his shock troops. Pivoting, the soldier directed a stream of 9 mm parabellum manglers at the enemy on his rear. He glimpsed Ulyatin holding her turf with a mask of savage intent, her M-16 all but disemboweling two Sikh fanatics, hurling them back in a shower of crimson.

As lead whined and sparked, searching him out, Bolan slid into a doorway across the hall, holding back the Uzi's trigger. Their Sikh allies were hurling lead death, obliterating bearded faces into pulpy goo. Unfortunately Bolan saw their Sikh comrades take the full lead brunt in the chest during the lightning toe-to-toe encounter. Those men were pinned to the wall from the lead hurricane but managed to empty their clips, taking out another fanatic, before they slid to ground, twitching in death throes.

One final sweep from his Uzi and Bolan tallied up two more of the enemy on his death march, driving them into tangled heaps on the floor. He slapped a fresh magazine into his Uzi. A quick look at Ulyatin found her somehow miraculously unscathed as she popped home a new magazine into her assault rifle.

An explosion from somewhere at the west end of the temple alerted Bolan to the new danger of the enemy unleashing RPG payloads, even if it meant bringing down the whole temple on their skulls. Crouched low, the enemy guns suddenly more concerned with their rear than their flanks, Bolan spotted the pall of smoke roiling over the barking weapons, marking Shiva's position. The Sikh who had loosed that RPG warhead was already bowled down by scissoring fingers of lead doom.

But it was the sudden and hasty fighting exit of five turbaned fanatics that snared Bolan's attention. In flight, the five blazed away with autofire at Shiva and his troops, then vanished around the north wall. Their vanishing act told the soldier they were moving east, his way.

Without glancing at Ulyatin, the Executioner surged past the sprawled dead, hell-bent on intercepting the Sikhs. Were they running, or were they seeking to lure them into a confined, even an open area where they could unleash RPG doomsday?

Bolan pulled the pin on his next-to-last frag grenade.

It was then the soldier got lucky. Through the fading rattle of autofire, he heard them calling out to one another.

Strained his hearing, and caught two names: Adjan, Maraka. Alive and well. Strangely enough there was no fear in their voices as they barked some plan at each other in their own tongue. No, there was some savage intent on their minds. It came through, loud and clear, in Bolan's combat-electrified senses.

The soldier hit the edge of the wall where it rounded to the north and peered around the corner. Right away AK-47s chased him to cover, but not before he tossed the bomb, dead center among the enemy.

The steel egg blew with a hellish peal of thunder. Breaking cover, Uzi fanning the killzone, Bolan found the detonation had shredded the tightly packed force. Still, in the corner of his eye, he sighted the tail-end flight of one Sikh who escaped ground zero, turban gone and body sailing out the main entrance.

The Executioner could only hope.

What he found were two Sikhs, crawling through their blood and scrabbling for weapons.

The soldier pinned them with unforgiving bursts where they crawled.

Now to find out who had gone airborne out the temple.

MCNEARY TALLIED the score. The visiting team was winning, but it wasn't over. Mop-up detail was taking place beyond the east wall. Pollock was over there, giving chase, cutting off the Sikh withdrawal.

Only moments ago, McNeary had seen the half-dozen Sikhs bolt from the prayer chamber. Caught up in the frenzy of battle, taking out the Sikhs trapped in the middle of the prayer chamber, McNeary never got off a shot at the fleeing terrorists. They were running, but he couldn't help but feel they had something in mind. Tucking tail and going underground, worming their way out of the temple through some secret passageway...well, it didn't strike him as the Sikh thing to do. The enemy had gone out hard, no hint of doing anything other than giving death or taking it. Why do anything different now?

Right now there were concentrated bursts of autofire following on the thunderclap of a frag bomb McNeary had glimpsed Pollock dropping into the retreating Sikhs. It all happened in the blink of an eye, but McNeary caught sight of flying bodies and shredded body parts riding the fireball.

McNeary understood the colonel's objective for this hit on the temple. He also wouldn't deny or begrudge the ballsy colonel the right to claim the heads of the Sikhs who had turned a quiet stretch of morning-rush-hour traffic into their personal highway of slaughter. Hell, no, McNeary wanted Pollock to do what had to be done. He only hoped those directly responsible for the murder and mayhem on American soil were either among the dead or right now on the run, into Pollock's death sights.

His M-16 up and ready, McNeary rolled into the middle of the prayer chamber. At first glance, nothing moved, just the final spasms of dead men, twitching it out.

"Peterson bought it."

McNeary turned, saw Barber with Peterson draped over his shoulder, blood spattering the marble floor. The CIA agent gave Peterson's shattered face a quick look, found he'd taken a Sikh slug right between the eyes. Even though he was numbed by the hard reality of having already lost a lot of men, McNeary still experienced a stab of anger. There wouldn't be any after-action reports when this was over, no one over him prepared to chew him out for the fiasco in the gorge, but that didn't make it any easier for McNeary to deal with the fact that he'd lost too damn many fighting men. Hell, most of these guys, he knew, didn't even have families or loved one back in the States who'd mourn their deaths. It was a shitty life.

"Watch yourselves on the way out," McNeary told his survivors.

Then he checked his watch. Just about time to fly.

He swept a gaze over the slaughter one last time, something warning McNeary that this was merely a prelude to some real ugliness in Mother Russia.

WITH THE WORLD coming to him through a shattered mist, Adjan couldn't be one hundred percent certain what had happened, didn't even know exactly where he was at the moment. But he knew it wasn't good. None of it.

Fear and anger cleared the cobwebs what seemed like an eternity later. Somehow he picked himself up on his hands and knees. Tasting the blood running down his face and into his mouth, it came back to him. The raid, all of them trapped in the middle of the prayer chamber, enemies coming at them from all directions, it had seemed. He had wanted a fight, one last stand to ensure his glory. One look at the invaders and he knew they were fighting, dying at the hands of Americans, armed with M-16 assault rifles. That alone had told him all he needed to know. So he had been tracked to the Punjab, hunted down like an animal for his mission in America.

When it had gone sour in the temple, Adjan recalled having to adjust to the situation, improvise, come up with something fast or they would all die in the M-16 cross fire. The idea had been to draw the invaders into giving chase. Once he had them in close, packed tight, he would destroy them all with one well-placed RPG warhead.

So much for that plan.

Out of nowhere, a tall man with an Uzi and with the coldest, most determined eyes Adjan had ever seen had shot up, blown apart what had to be left of his fellow Sikh warriors. At the last split second, Adjan remembered spotting the grenade, running for the arched entrance, only to be lifted off his feet and hurled by the blast.

The haze was gone now. Adjan saw the villagers,

a sea of angry faces gathered beyond the front wall. Traitors. Why didn't they charge the temple, kill the enemy with their bare hands if they had to?

"Maraka? Or is it Adjan?"

Before he even turned his head to locate the source of the voice, Adjan knew it was the tall American with the Uzi and the cold eyes. The voice seemed to strike Adjan from some great distance, or call to him from the bottom of a tomb. Maybe even beckon him on into eternity.

Blood stinging into his eyes, Adjan slowly swiveled his head. The American came straight out of the drifting tendrils of smoke and cordite, out of the gloom of the arched door and into the light.

In the corner of his eye, Adjan made out the shape of his AK-47. For some reason, he knew he would never reach the weapon in time, grimly aware he was about to die, executed in the courtyard of the temple as if he were nothing more than some sick animal that had to be put to sleep. The thought never even whispered through his mind to ask the stranger to spare his life.

"I am Mokhan Singh Adjan. I am Lion."

"The lion is done roaring for the day. Consider this your final driving lesson. I've got your permit right here."

The American pulled the biggest pistol Adjan had ever seen, was lining it up for his face when the Sikh clawed for the AK-47.

"I'VE GOT YOUR PERMIT right here."

It wasn't any attempt at morbid humor, nor was

he taunting or mocking the Sikh butcher locked in his grim death sights. No, the words rose up on their own, came from nowhere out of the steel and fire gripping his soul.

All Bolan was seeking was positive confirmation of a prime target.

In short order, the guy gave it to him.

The Uzi's clip was empty, and Bolan opted to unleather the .44 Magnum Desert Eagle, which seemed to have a life of its own as it filled his hand. The enemy was vanquished, and the soldier would have no need for rapid-fire autopower in the immediate present.

The future, of course, was something else altogether.

At that moment, the Executioner was vaguely aware of the Sikh masses beyond the wall. Somewhere beyond his bleeding, squirming but defiant prey, the soldier managed to read the silence and the stillness of the villagers as some sort of acceptance of the inevitable. Perhaps some of them had cheered, congratulated Maraka and Adjan on their bloody return home to the Punjab. Perhaps not. As long as no one in the mob offered to become armed sacrificial lambs, well, Bolan was content to let the villagers of Abutani go on with life as normal. Undoubtedly the Indian army would be marching into the Punjab in due order. If there were fanatics who had gone to ground, escaped the soldier's brand of ultimate justice, then he had to believe the legitimate Indian authorities would hunt them down and take them, in or out.

No matter.

The terrorist who had ruined countless innocent lives in a span of eternal horrifying minutes was at the Executioner's foot.

Adjan hauled in the AK-47.

Bolan stroked the hand cannon's trigger, rode out the recoil to a peal of thunder, cored the hollowpoint slug just above the bridge of Adjan's nose. There was no need for a second round.

A moment later, rotor wash broke through the trailing echo of the killing shot. The gunship touched down near the front wall. The ensuing dust storm drove the Sikh masses down the street.

"You can be sure we won't be seeing any Sikh terrorists coming to America. Not anytime soon."

Bolan acknowledged Shiva's cryptic-sounding remark with a passing steely gaze as CIA forces approached from the rear.

Ulyatin spoke up next, her face a hard mask of grim determination. "All right, Colonel, you got what you wanted here. Now, allow me to go and take what I need."

13

The nagging doubt and grim concern were taxing his frayed nerves with each hour that dragged by.

Langston gave their not too shabby accommodations an approving eye, more for the effect of a hidden camera than anything else. He had to stay suspicious, keep his guard up, braced for the worst.

As soon as the Antonovs touched down at the remote Tajikistan installation, a cadre of armed, grim-faced hardmen he'd never seen before had whisked them off to their quarters at the south end of the main complex. But not before they had been relieved of their weapons.

Outside, full night had descended over the rugged steppe of the southern frontier near the Afghan border. Beyond the silent treatment on the tarmac—where he'd parted company with the GRU major and his Spetsnaz survivors—Langston had been surprised he wasn't greeted with the bone-chilling cold of Russia's Old Man Winter he had anticipated. Sure, snow blanketed the steppe for as far as the eye could see, but he figured it was only a few degrees below freezing at worst. Apparently the real ugly weather was farther north. As in Moscow and vicinity.

That began bringing to mind the main problem of

the main event. A history buff, Langston couldn't help but feel the ghosts of Napoleon or the Wehrmacht when those armies had made their big move on Moscow, only to be primarily beaten by the scourge of nature. Of course, the tenacity of the Russian foot soldier had something to do with turning the tide, but when a man was freezing to death, fighting was the last thing on his mind. Unless, of course, that man figured a surge of adrenaline in the face of mortal combat would warm him up.

Well, a lot still remained to be seen about the main event, as far as he was concerned. For starters, details were sketchy, but he knew what the principle objective was: a Kremlin takedown.

He poured himself another vodka from the wet bar, topped it off with grapefruit. He fired up a cigarette, then observed his men. In silence, they were finishing up some fat plates heaped with filet mignon, potatoes and some kind of stew. Vodka all around, but he'd warned them go easy on the hard stuff. Silence was also imperative. The latest in state-of-the-art listening devices or cameras could be anywhere, invisible even to a scathing and trained eye.

Langston leaned on the bar, working on his smoke and vodka. He belched, was reminded he had a belly full of some of the sweetest filet he'd had in years. Were they lambs being fattened for the slaughter?

The problem of the main event, right. Undoubtedly the Council was right now putting the final touches on the mission, maneuvering the right people in place. All in all, it was insane, perhaps even suicidal, storming the Kremlin for a changing of the guard.

Even if they succeeded, what then? Controlling Russia was a logistical nightmare in and of itself. No czar ever really did it; even Stalin had a full plate keeping the masses in line under his iron hand. Just for starters, it was more than six thousand miles from the Baltic Sea to the Bering Strait. Tack on three thousand miles north to south, from the Arctic Circle to the Pamirs, and you were looking at the largest land mass of any one country on earth. Not to mention that the far frontiers bordered forty percent of Europe and Asia, or that there were more than one hundred ethnic groups all over the map, most of them armed, all of them hungry and at odds with whoever might be in power...a logistical nightmare, damn right. One that could *only* be nipped in the bud by armed and brutal force.

In short, Russia was a mess. Communism, Langston knew, had never really died. Rather, it had gone to ground. An army of hard-line Communists was out there, waiting, honing its blades, ready to seize the day of its return to triumph, power. When the Berlin Wall fell, all the bleeding hearts and do-gooder peacocks in the District of Clowns had shouted for joy that the Big Bear was going democratic, and what a beautiful thing that was. Cold war over, new markets to consume American goods. Right. No one had seemed either capable or strong enough to read the writing on the wall.

History had time and again proved that drastic overnight change never worked. All Langston had to do was look at the horrific scope of potential Armageddon-like problems now plaguing Russia when

Ivan had supposedly lowered his hammer and sickle: unemployed, starving masses; crime, the likes of which Russia had never seen, stepping in to pave the way for economic reform; alcoholism skyrocketing; suicide a national epidemic, marauding gangs of thieves, murderers and rapists stalking the streets of every major city; the new military in total disarray.

And the West kept pouring money into Russia, which, Langston knew, only fueled the fires of rampant corruption. Maybe this was democracy, after all.

Indeed, over the past several hours, there had been plenty of time to look at the past, dwell on the present, worry about the future.

Too much time. The bottom line was Langston wanted to bail. The problem was getting his hands on the rest of his money. For damn sure, there could be no graceful way to put it to the Council, but there were enough former Company power players among the men, and hopefully they would understand his predicament. A simple "I want my money, I'm gone, you're on your own" should do it. Beyond that, well, if things got unreasonable, he would take his chances. First, he had to meet with the Council. Second, he had to get his hands on some firepower.

Langston went through another vodka and three more cigarettes, then the door opened. The sight of Major Slobovka striding into the room, sporting a grim smile, as if he were enjoying some private joke, made Langston's heart skip a beat. Slobovka had changed into a sweater and pants, but still wore the same combat boots, all in black. Seeing the major was unarmed put Langston's mind a little at ease.

"I am here to report that there is good news and there is bad news."

Langston gritted his teeth, but choked down his anger. "Skip the drama. Let's have it."

"The good news is we are set to go tomorrow. The key individuals are in place in Moscow and are awaiting their orders from the Council. All of us will be thoroughly briefed, just after dawn. I suggest all of you get a good night's sleep."

When the major paused, Langston was set to erupt. "And what's the bad news?"

Slobovka's expression hardened. "You will not receive the rest of your payment until the successful completion of our mission."

Langston wondered if the major was lying, taunting him to get a reaction. Calm, Langston said, "I want a face-to-face with my people."

"They are all our people, Comrade Langston. And I am afraid that is impossible."

"You mean we're confined to quarters until they see fit to call us?"

"Precisely. They are working around-the-clock to seal the final stage. They cannot be disturbed."

Langston sounded a grim chuckle. "You ever think, Major, that we, like the Sikhs, are sacrificial lambs? That maybe this is strictly geared as a suicide mission so the big shots can make their statement, shake things up all over your Mother Russia?"

"I would put caution in your words, Comrade. If what you say is true, and I do not believe that, then, well, I will be by your side when we act. Now, if that is all, you will excuse me."

Slobovka left Langston seething. Alone, he gave each of his men in turn "the look." In turn, each of his men nodded. There. It was settled. If they were going to die in Russia, the least they could do was to die for themselves. Not to mention taking out Slobovka and as many Spetsnaz fighters as they could. If the Council was going to piss on his dreams, then Langston was going to fling some back in their faces.

"ARE WE CLEAR on all of this, people?"

They sat amidships, gathered under the soft, ghostly orange-yellow glow of the overhead lights for the final brief. In hard silence, Bolan worked on a cup of coffee, listening without seeming to listen to Mr. Hammer. Other than the cold facts of the hard hit on the enemy's secret base in Tajikistan, the Executioner wasn't clear on too much. For starters, Mr. Hammer had bulled in right off with his satellite-recon photos, grid maps and intel, his bulldog face scowling from the outset, putting angry, piercing blue eyes on any and everyone. Exactly who and what Mr. Hammer was, Bolan could only venture a good guess. More heavy hitters from the Company's special operations, principally black operations.

The backup team comprised twenty-four hard-eyed, grim-faced commandos with M-16s with M-203 grenade launchers mounted under the barrels. Everyone now donned black parkas for the night hit. From time to time, Mr. Hammer addressed his people as Mr. Sickle, Mr. Reaper, Mr. Plow and so on. And Bolan got the distinct impression Shiva had been relieved of command. But exactly where the chain of command led, the Executioner wasn't sure, nor did it really matter. What was important was the soldier was still part of the team, in there for the final stretch of what Mr. Hammer had code-named as Operation Bearhug.

Just as important, Bolan had been assigned to ride it out with Shiva, his five and Ulyatin. Since, as Mr. Hammer had put it, those who had already worked together should stick together, Bolan was destined to hit the south end of the base with the players he'd run with so far. That was good enough for him. Shiva, his men and Ulyatin had proved their mettle, all of them bonded in the blood of battle. There was no sense in shaking up the program now.

The rumble of the AC-130 gunship's engines in his ears, Bolan figured they'd been in the air a good four hours. It wouldn't be long now. The soldier gave the plan a quick review, then assessment. Mr. Hammer and his people would parachute in on the complex at the north side first, plant the time-delayed four hundred pounds of C-4. The Spectre would swing south, where Bolan and his fighting half would drop in by parachute, get busy clamping the pincer attack on the enemy.

On the surface, the plan seemed solid enough, but there were factors Bolan didn't like. The complex was floodlit, with antiaircraft batteries on the north and south ends. There were two large barracks for the troops and no clear fix on enemy numbers. According to the combined intel of Shiva, Mr. Hammer and Ulyatin, they figured they'd be looking at a hundred Spetsnaz commandos on the ground. Six helicopter gunships stood on the tarmac, beside another dozen armored fighting vehicles. Fuel bins were near the airstrip, with open ground all around the hardsite. Bolan could count on radar most likely picking up their advance, no matter how low the gunship flew. Given what had happened in India, Bolan could be sure Slobovka would have the base on full alert.

"You have a problem with any of this, Colonel? Speak up, you're among friends here."

Bolan met Mr. Hammer's cold gaze. The soldier took his time responding.

"Two items," the Executioner said. "One, I get the impression this is strictly search-and-destroy."

"So, what's the problem?"

"If that's the plan, use this gunship on the complex before we hit the ground. If we're looking at facing off with a hundred-strong or more Spetsnaz, then we'll need every possible edge we can get. Item number two—the charges. Where are you going to set them and what's the time delay before we can expect four hundred pounds of C-4 to knock out half the base?"

Mr. Hammer held his ground, let the silence drag. He squared his shoulders, sucked in a deep breath, thrust his hands on his hips.

The Executioner sipped his coffee, waiting. He wasn't looking to put the man on the spot, usurp whatever authority Mr. Hammer had over the operation. No, Bolan just wanted some solid answers, simply because he wasn't hell-bent on committing suicide when they were plunging for the compound.

Finally Mr. Hammer chuckled grimly. "I understand, Colonel, you and the others here we had to evacuate because you struck out on your own. Well, it caused me to alter the game plan in order to bail you out. It meant risking aborting the entire mission. You got your Sikh piece of flesh, now let me make something perfectly clear." He paused to let the edge in his voice sink in, then went on. "Myself and my people have been forced to wait in the wings for the word to move ahead with Operation Bearhug. We are not backup, we are not the second team, we are not intelligence agents who dance around in the shadows and play the finer art of espionage. We, in short, are the heavy hitters, the cleanup crew. I admit you and the others have played no small part, but right now you are strictly part of my team. We are going in hard. We shoot, blow up, rip out throats by bare hand, if necessary, anything that moves on that base. Now, the obvious question you might want to ask is, if we are so critical to the success of this operation, then why weren't we here at the start of this fiasco. I have a simple answer of 'I don't know.' I take my orders, and I carry them out.

"To answer your questions, Colonel. Item one, my gunship crew is ordered to return one full hour after we hit the ground. I feel an air attack would take away our initial moment of surprise on the ground. I need those charges planted. Further, I want eye-to-eye contact with the enemy when we engage because it is the only way I can confirm a body count. With those ZSU cannons on the ground, I can't see the point in risking one of them blowing my bird out of the sky before we get this thing in gear. By the remote chance that does happen, we'll use one of the Russian transport planes to get us back to base in India. As for the charges, once planted, they'll be timed to go off in fifteen seconds. Meaning we are forced to keep moving. No standoffs, no getting pinned down. Now, are there any other questions?''

Bolan answered by breaking eye contact and falling back into grim silence. Okay, the man was going to have it his way or no way, no matter what. In effect, it all struck the soldier as a planned suicide mission. If they made it out of Russia, then fine. If not...well, that wasn't good enough for Bolan—no, it wasn't even in his game plan. He needed to get to the head cannibals of this renegade intelligence conspiracy. If he didn't, there was no telling where the conspiracy would lead next. Perhaps a neighboring Arab country? Syria? Iran? Iraq? The Russians had been arming those countries for years. But who was to say they hadn't decided to up the ante somehow, call in the markers?

Certainly Slobovka and his murderous Company renegades had proved they could train and mobilize a small army of seething malcontents, then turn them loose on a target.

All along Bolan had known but not accepted his role as a shooter on the periphery of the operation, along for the ride as an added gun. Naturally Brognola had used his clout and contacts to land him in-country, then link him up with the clandestine strike force. But too much had happened since his ominous face-to-face with Smith in Virginia. Too many riddles, too many unanswered questions.

It was set to erupt. Critical mass.

That was good enough for the Executioner.

Once on the ground and geared up in attack mode, the soldier would do what he did best: seek and engage, search and destroy.

Bolan gave Shiva, then Ulyatin a narrow-eyed search. He wondered what was going through the woman's mind, now that Slobovka appeared up for grabs. First come, first served. If she didn't settle her personal vendetta, Bolan decided that was merely another aggravating circumstance that would play out in short order. The woman sat there in brooding silence.

It was Shiva's frown, shrug of the shoulders and the spark of empathy in the man's eyes that surprised Bolan for a moment. But the soldier understood. They were a team, together, bonded from the killing fields. Shiva's silent message to him was to let it ride. So be it.

Once again the Executioner restrained himself from checking his watch. A passenger more than once aboard fixed-wing gunships, he knew the AC-130 Spectre was a convoy killer, complete with four 20 mm cannons and four 7.62 mm miniguns. Damn right, he knew the Spectre should be used on the hardsite to soften it up, but it wasn't his call. But they had picked the right warbird. He placed the Spectre's top cruising speed at 375 miles per hour, knew the mammoth warbird held the world's record for staying up in the air, the longest military flight logged at 29.7 hours. Plenty of speed and fuel to get them there—and maybe back. It nagged him it was a shameful waste of firepower. He could also be certain two 20 mm Vulcan cannons, fixed to the wings, were proved to pound out 2,500 rounds a minute. Tack on one 40 mm Bofors cannon, a 105 mm howitzer mounted beside it, and it was all he could do to keep from slapping some sense into Mr. Hammer. But if it was a stealthy advance on the hardsite they were seeking, then they could rely on the Spectre's state-of-the-art global inertial navigation and radar, infrared and low-light tracking systems. Even still...

The game plan didn't suit Bolan. All in all, they would get there when they got there. Looking left, he saw the chute packs, strung out in a neat line, right in front of two large crates.

As if reading his mind, Mr. Hammer's gruff voice invaded Bolan's solemn privacy.

"Colonel, Shiva and the rest of you people. If you want to pick out some additional firepower, feel free to go through my stockpile. There's both fragmentation and incendiary grenades, just for starters."

Mr. Hammer proceeded to inform Colonel Pollock he might consider replacing his Israeli machine pistol with an M-16 with attached M-203 grenade launcher. Glancing at the guy who had rolled in and pretty much knocked Shiva aside, Bolan was tempted to tell the man it was the best idea he'd heard yet, but said nothing. Either way, the soldier intended to take what he wanted from those crates.

Ever since Mr. Hammer had first opened his

mouth, it hit Bolan more than ever that the real plus was that his team was on their own.

Instinct warned the Executioner it was destined to go down bad.

IT ALL WENT TO HELL right off.

No sooner had Hammer and his people jumped off than Bolan detected the faint sounds of autofire, then the heavy boom of explosions pealed through the open fuselage doorway. The Spectre was coming out of its port-side bank, rumbling on its straight line to off-load the second team at the southern end of the complex, when the pilot's voice started barking over the intercom.

"Go, go!"

No one had to be told even the first time to hit the door. Shiva's commandos, then Ulyatin were forging into the wind howling through the doorway when the explosions took on closing thunder. It was the ZSU cannons, hard at work, Bolan knew.

Chute pack on, hooked up to the static line, the Executioner had been designated by Mr. Hammer to be the last one out the door. The soldier's M-16 with attached M-203 grenade launcher hung by a leather strap down his side, allowing him quick access to the assault rifle while working the risers. Pockets stuffed with six frag grenades, his parka unzipped halfway down to allow a swift hand for the spare clips and 40 mm grenades for the M-203, or the .44 Magnum Desert Eagle in shoulder holster, Bolan was set to go, jump for the final killing ground.

Shiva, next-to-last in line, threw Bolan a grim look

over his shoulder. While the pilot's voice took on a note of mounting urgency, Shiva told him, "Good luck, Colonel. See you on the ground."

Shiva was gone.

And the Executioner hurled himself through the doorway, not a second too soon.

In the next heartbeat, the sky flashed and thundered above Bolan. He was free-falling on the start of the six-hundred-foot combat jump, tracer rounds from the ZSU at the far north end of the compound streaking past him, when the tracking hellfire raked the Spectre. In the corner of his eye, as the aircraft attempted to go south, Bolan glimpsed the behemoth gunship being vaporized by a marching line of mushrooming fireballs.

So much for any air support.

As if giant fists were slamming him in the back, the shock waves propelled Bolan toward white-carpeted earth. Awash for dangerous heartbeats in the brilliant glow of firelight, he knew he was a falling target, soon to become a hovering man-bird to possibly be plucked out of the sky. Already he saw the enemy racing from the south end of the complex, on the run for the other ZSU-23-4. The imminent danger was twofold. First, opening the chute would send him skyward to be shredded by any falling wreckage. Second the enemy soldiers, now fanning the compound, searching for targets with their assault rifles, were certain to spot him as he dropped for their position.

There was no choice to make.

Bolan pulled the rip cord and was lurched skyward, his ears filled with the thunderous explosions above, but luckily it sounded as if the Spectre had gone far enough south from his position to spare him the fiery holocaust. Falling wreckage went south also.

Then Bolan found the enemy had spotted his falling form.

It was going to be a hard landing, if he landed at all.

He angled for the antiaircraft cannon, then let go of the risers, lifting the M-16.

14

They were off the couch, leaping off beds and rolling for the door after the first distant rumble of thunder.

Langston knew there was no mistaking that sound, knew exactly what was happening. They were under attack.

Beyond the walls of their quarters, he clearly made out the relentless chatter of autofire, then the mighty peal of some monstrous blast from some point south and above seemed ready to come crashing down through the ceiling. The lingering detonation from the sky was muffled in the next moment as he heard the series of blasts, coming from the north wing, shock waves rippling under his feet with steady and angry force.

Langston had a bellyful of rage, now edged with fear, topped with a savage instinct to survive. He was angry at being snubbed by the Council, but that was just for openers. Second, and worst of all, he was seething over the fact he wasn't going to see the rest of his money. Unless, of course, he licked the Council's boots, tapped their dance. Finally his fury now reached volcanic potential by this sudden stark reality they were being hit hard and no one had seen fit to arm him and his people.

Well, it was time to turn the rage on any and all comers. In short, time to fly in one of the Antonovs. Anyone who stood in their way was dead meat. The Council, Spetsnaz, whoever the hell was hitting them, it didn't matter.

Just to make certain his men were crystal clear on all of this, he turned at the door, growled, "Play it straight until we get our hands on some firepower. Then we go for broke. We're out of here."

Bursting out into the hallway, Langston spotted ten Spetsnaz commandos in black, toting AK-47s. They were on the move from the north end when they stopped beneath one of the half-dozen cameras mounted on the ceiling, beside a white door with an iron-barred window. Langston didn't see Slobovka.

"Hey, you want to tell me what the hell is going on?" Langston snarled, moving for the commandos, his men in lockstep, flanks and rear. He hoped one of the Russians spoke English.

One of them did, but gave Langston a mocking grin and some smart mouth. "We are under attack, what does it sound like to you?"

Another explosion rocked the building as a commando slipped a key into the door.

"You care to let us join the action, mister?" Langston growled.

The Spetsnaz commando with the smart mouth jabbed a finger to the side, pointing down an adjacent west wall. "Second door down. You find what you need. Then join us. Move!"

Langston made his move for that room, all right. Inside he found exactly what they needed. He picked up an AK-47 and stuffed his waistband with spare clips. In grim silence, he and his men ventured back out into the hall. For a frozen moment, Langston was surprised to find the Russians hauling Major Thornton from the cell; he was certain they would have disposed of the man after he'd served his purpose on the glacier. Not so. Thornton was now intended to serve as some kind of bargaining chip against the invaders. It wasn't going to work the second time around.

Langston waited until the Spetsnaz fighters looked his way, then he cut loose with his AK-47, holding back the trigger for full-auto slaughter. Pros that they were, his men flanked him, joined the massacre. Merciless streams of tracking lead swept the Spetsnaz force, back and forth, scythed through them, cut them down, chopped them up. Langston didn't spare Major Thornton, either. They didn't stop until they had expended every last round in their clips, until there was nothing left in that hallway but twitching limbs and white walls running red.

PLUMMETING AT FOURTEEN feet per second, Bolan locked his sights on the enemy. A quick head count, and he saw at least six shadows, armed with AK-47s and attempting to man the ZSU-23-4. They never made it.

No sooner did the enemy swing weapons for his falling form than Bolan triggered a 40 mm HE grenade into the pack. Closing on the Spetsnaz hardforce from a southwest angle, the Executioner narrowly escaped the shock of the ground-zero blast.

Still, two Russian fighters staggered from the smoke
and flames. A lightning 3-round burst from Bolan's
M-16 drove one commando to blood-drenched snow.
The other Spetsnaz fighter broke the soldier's rapid
descent, more by chance than design. Smashing his
boots off the commando's chin, Bolan caught the
sickening crack of bone just before he touched down,
hard, tucked and rolled. When he came up, shucking
off the pack, he found his human LZ was right then
hammering to earth on the end of his unexpected
flight. A quick check of the unmoving form revealed
that Bolan had broken the man's neck.

Then he took in the hellgrounds. At the moment,
the raging battle looked confined to the north end.
There, explosions blossomed around the airfield, the
wreckage of helicopter gunships riding the crests of
fiery mushroom clouds. Next, the north face of the
complex was obliterated by what the soldier could
only assume was a massive C-4 detonation.

Judging the furious counterattack by a small army
of black-suited Spetsnaz commandos, Bolan knew
the war had only just begun. Once again he could
find fault with Mr. Hammer's bullheaded strategy.
Black parkas against blacksuit meant panicky trigger
fingers by men consumed in the heat of a fight to the
death could just as easily spell doom by friendly fire.

But Bolan was on his own. A glimpse at the mountains of flaming wreckage to the south, where the
Spectre's debris had crushed some structure, told him
none of them might leave Russia alive.

Another hard surveillance of the killing grounds
gave testament that Mr. Hammer and his people were

the ones taking the hammering. The tarmac where the Antonovs were grounded and still intact, and the fifty-yard stretch of no-man's-land between the barracks to the west and the main complex were littered with black parkas still in harness and chutes billowing. At his first and only look at their casualties, Bolan figured they'd lost ten, maybe more to Spetsnaz guns. Descending toward the compound, those men had been shot up in harness, most likely spotted then locked in Spetsnaz gun sights by the series of floodlights bathing the compound. Factor in the firelight from explosions, and no fighter on either side would be safe for long if he held his ground.

On the move for the doorway at the south end, Bolan found the main complex was much larger from an up-close ground perspective. It ran a good quarter mile, north to south, the same length east to west. And there was no telling how many enemy guns he would have to confront once inside.

Closing on the door, Bolan suddenly spotted a figure surging across the roof of the barracks. A moment later, that figure was blazing away with an M-16, firing down with long, sweeping bursts of relentless 5.56 mm lead death, cracking open the skulls of Spetsnaz commandos who were pouring from the building. Another explosion flashed to the north, washing a band of firelight over the barracks, offering Bolan a fleeting glimpse of Shiva's mask of grim determination. Shiva cracked a fresh clip into his assault rifle, held his ground from his vantage point atop the barracks and went back to his deadly chore.

As Bolan hit the corner of the main complex,

Shiva was lost to sight. Reaching the door, the Executioner then heard the sudden and long roar of autofire, coming from some point well inside the building. But the sound of men cursing and screaming in horrible agony was unmistakable.

A slaughter was taking place inside the building.

Reloading his M-203, the Executioner grasped the doorknob, braced for anything, steeled to deliver lightning death.

It was every man for himself.

SUCCESS WOULD ONLY COME the hard way, and McNeary knew that meant wiping out every last enemy there, or die trying. Either way, it had become a crapshoot. No doubt, the base had been on full alert, radar had most likely picked them up and Spetsnaz had been ready to greet them.

As soon as he had landed on the roof of the barracks, the pack was off and McNeary was on the hunt. Autofire was splitting the air all over the base, with ear-shattering explosions peppering the airfield, reducing gunships to smoking scrap. From his rooftop vantage point, he could see what was left of Hammer's people planting charges at the north end of the main complex. Their M-16s were spraying at any Spetsnaz shadow that moved. But the enemy had taken concealment in doorways, up and down the west side of the main building, leapfrogging ahead for the airfield. In short, Hammer and his force were set to get pinned down.

Whatever was to happen next, McNeary knew it would far exceed the moment of near death he'd escaped during the drop. Even then, he could still hear the bullets whizzing past his ears, puncturing his chute only seconds before he hit the roof. It became obvious with a quick look at the bodies in harness all over the ground that Hammer's people had fared the worst. Hell, the Spetsnaz killers had been presented with a hovering shooting gallery of human birds.

The upshot was that the colonel had landed.

On the run, M-16 in hand, McNeary caught a moment's glimpse of Pollock, the colonel now surging for the south end of the main complex on the heels of his fiery touchdown. The colonel was either one lucky SOB, McNeary thought, or the man was blessed by a little divine helping hand. When the Spectre had been vaporized, right over their heads, fear had stabbed McNeary in the heart like a knife. It had been a damn close shave.

But somehow they made the ground.

McNeary only hoped he got the chance to clear himself with Pollock later. All along, he'd known who and what Hammer and his people were. And those guys were no backup players, no second-string assassins. No, sir, those guys were the Company's top assassins, the mad dogs on a short leash. Life, not even their own, meant spit to them. But given the fiascos that had dogged them during the mission so far, how would it wash with Colonel Pollock if he'd known a suicide force was waiting in the wings, chomping at the bit to kick some serious ass, even if it meant all of them died in Russia?

Suddenly McNeary realized he was alone on the

roof. He wondered if his own men, and Ulyatin, had survived the drop. Then he heard the shooting, coming from beyond the south end of the barracks, and he had to assume he wasn't completely on his own. Not yet.

Below, he found them racing out of the barracks, unaware for the moment that he was right over them. McNeary cut loose with lead death from above. Heads erupted in pink clouds of flying blood. Backs were ripped open by the merciless 5.56 mm barrage, from the base of the spine to shoulders. He mowed them down where they stood, then adjusted his aim, lifted the M-16 and pumped a 40 mm grenade toward the main complex. The ensuing blast took out at least three shadows who had been blazing away with AK-47s from a doorway.

Out of nowhere, a line of slugs started punching divots in the snow to his right flank. Unable to determine where the tracking lead was coming from, McNeary darted from the edge, started running for the south end when a volcanic eruption of fire demolished the north side of the barracks. A moment later, another fireball took to the air.

The next thing McNeary knew he was airborne, heard then felt screaming tongues of fire on his backside.

THE COUNCIL'S ORDERS were explicit—find them a hostage. Not just Major Thornton, but take one of the invaders alive, bring him to the war room.

Slobovka was coming out of the surveillance room, en route to attempt to do precisely that when it seemed as if the entire north wing was coming down on his head. The tremendous explosion obliterated the north wall, hurling concrete, smoke and fire straight at him, but Slobovka was already throwing himself back into the surveillance room, hugging the facade of terminals that monitored the south perimeter. Already his troops were surging past the room, firing on the run, against the mystery force. It then sounded as if the entire compound was rocked by the endless thunder and earthquakelike tremors of countless more explosions.

He had been ordered to crush the invasion, fight to the last man, if necessary. He didn't see the sense in cursing the men of the Council, but he couldn't help but resent the fact they were safe and secure, bunkered underground.

Slobovka then saw something on the monitor that held him fascinated for several moments. A lone invader was parachuting down on the ZSU cannon at the south edge. He couldn't be certain, but the way the man fought and moved, he would bet his life it was the commando from the glacier who had killed so many of his Spetsnaz troops. Interesting. And now that lone invader was moving on the south end of the building.

Slobovka barked for two of his commandos to follow him. He took three gas masks from a hidden wall compartment, handed one each to his commandos, then snugged on the last one.

Swiftly Slobovka led his commandos down the hall, south, cut a corner. He was marching west in the wing that housed the interrogation rooms, prisoner quarters and armory when he heard the sudden and extended barking of automatic weapons. He came to a sudden halt at the end of the hall, witnessed the last of the commandos he had sent to round up Major Thornton topple in a lifeless sprawl. Rage seized Slobovka when he saw it was Langston and his thugs who had butchered his men and Major Thornton.

Slobovka snatched an AK-47 from one of his commandos, prepared to cut loose on their blindside when the treacherous assassins whirled, spotted him, then bolted out of sight. They were cowards, traitors, he thought, greedy thugs who had only been interested in money all along. He put them out of mind, grimly intent to deal with Langston and his criminals in short order. There was nowhere they could run, nowhere for them to hide.

Then the door at the far south end of the hall opened. Slobovka glanced up at the vent over the massacred bodies, before sliding out of sight as the invader ventured inside.

If nothing else, Slobovka had a hostage for the Council.

BOLAN KNEW he had stepped in on the tail end of a slaughter. The question was, who had massacred whom and why?

Crouched, closing the door behind him, the soldier padded up the hall. It was too quiet, too still all of a sudden. He saw the mounted cameras on both sides of the hall, blasted them to sparking ruins with short bursts from his M-16. Outside he heard the battle around the compound raging on.

When he closed on the bodies, Bolan spotted the red star on one commando's chest. He had seen this kind of brutal work before. Langston was somewhere in the building. Another look and Bolan found himself gazing into the vacant eyes of Major Thornton, the major's cuffed hands still twitching in the final spasms.

Bolan choked down his anger. He was checking his rear when he made out the soft hissing sound coming from above. Bolan looked up and spotted the vent, already feeling his legs turning to rubber. He started to move ahead, his legs growing heavier with each step, when he saw the entire hall was lined with vents on both sides. And he heard the same hissing of the colorless, odorless gas coming from each vent.

The Executioner thought he saw three figures emerge, wearing gas masks, but the world was suddenly shrinking into a gray haze.

Then everything went black.

15

The biting scent of ammonia brought Bolan around to grim reality. He came to with a lurch, survival instincts flaring. His first inclination was to strike back, fight like hell if this was the end. Then he saw the two shadows, bathed in white light, step back. The shadows had AK-47s pointed at his face. As the fog in his head started to clear, he realized he was alive for a reason.

He turned his head a little, and the harsh white light then pierced his eyes. He closed his eyes, reopened them, squinting to adjust to the glare. He was weak, his head was spinning and he was nauseous from the gas.

"What is your name?"

The voice seemed to come to Bolan straight from the light, miles away.

"Pollock. Colonel."

"Who do you work for? The CIA?"

"The United States government is who I work for."

"Very well. Do you know who we are, Colonel Pollock? Of course you don't. We are the most powerful men on the face of this planet. We are the Council for the New World Order."

There. It was all he wanted to know. He had arrived, a face-to-face with the head of the hydra. The soldier sucked in a deep breath through his nose, clearing his head. Slowly he clambered to his feet. Behind he saw the two Spetsnaz commandos flanking a door. They were close, but not close enough for Bolan to make a lunge for their throats. Facing front, he peered into the shimmering wall of white light.

They sat on a raised platform. With the bank of lights striking their backs, they were mere faceless shadows to Bolan. He found himself standing in the center of a semicircular table, behind which he counted eleven silhouettes. They were looking down on him, sitting in hard silence, as if judging him or weighing their options. Bolan heard a faint rumble from above. So, they were underground. How long he had been out, he couldn't be sure. Nor could he possibly assess how the battle above was going. Directly above the Council were banks of cameras. The soldier had to assume they knew how the fight was shaping up.

"I assume the obvious question you want to ask, Colonel, is why you're still alive."

"It crossed my mind. You want a hostage to make sure you get out of here in one piece. To carry on your New World Order."

"Not exactly, but it's all up to you. Before you get too carried away with your own self-importance, Colonel, allow me to make an analogy between the human race and the animal kingdom. Picture this. An African savanna, dominated by the mighty and fearless lion. One day, a lesser but no less fearless predator, the hyena, decides to encroach on the lion's territory. Hyena urinates on lion's turf, challenging the lion's right to dominance. Somewhat amused, lion does not strike back. Hyena spends much of the day, trotting around the savanna, feeling he's won something of the start of total victory. All the other animals watch, wonder why the lion does nothing. Hyena struts some more, urinates again near the lion. Do you know, Colonel, where I'm going with this?''

"Lion finally strikes back, chases down the hyena and breaks its neck. You're the lion, right.''

"And you, Colonel, are the hyena, pissing on our territory.''

"Let me guess. You want to recruit me.''

His vision fully cleared, Bolan had the voice pinned down to the shadow, right in front of him, sandwiched between five figures on both sides.

"Once again, that is entirely up to you.''

"You people act pretty damn confident you've got the situation under control.''

"We've taken heavy casualties, Colonel. Even still, we are prepared right now to launch the coup d'état to end all coup d'états. One radio call to Moscow and it begins.''

"It's a suicide mission. You might take down the Kremlin, even hold it for a while, but the Russian people, what you might refer to as the new military, won't sit on the sidelines and watch their country thrown back into militant communism.''

"Why wouldn't they? This country has a history of bloody revolution, of seizing the reins of power by brute force. Colonel, I have a small army in place, ready to move on our word.''

''And without you?''

''There is no way we can be defeated or deterred, Colonel. Not by you or anyone else. There are too many out there who believe as we do, who want what we want. With that knowledge in mind, I will tell you that without us, there can be no New World Order. Our people in place will merely resume their lives in the military and intelligence agencies as before. Some of them, of course, will be forced to ground.''

It was all Bolan needed to hear. It could end right there, but only if he acted.

''Who we are is not important. Rather it is *what* we are.''

''Which is what? Former disgruntled superspies from various intelligence agencies around the world?''

''We are far more than that, Colonel. For the past two decades, we have been the real power, but from the shadows. We have controlled, manipulated everything from proliferating the worldwide narcotics traffic in order to stabilize the world economy, to assassinations of heads of state, to overthrowing entire smaller but no less important countries in the world which the average person has never heard of. Many of us here have committed what would be called crimes by your politicians and your public at large. And all we did was carry out the orders from those in power who have everything to hide and to lose. They may have thought they played us as pawns, but we became the lions, they, the hyenas.''

Bolan found it all incredible. But it was plausible in the worst-case nightmare scenario, given what he knew about the power and potential ruthlessness of intelligence agencies, particularly those infrastructures that handled sensitive or black operations. Not to mention the savage nature of animal man in his never-sated hunger for power and dominance. And the soldier could be certain these savages had the necessary cash, clout and connections to sell their New World Order. In short, they were selling anarchy and death.

"You're telling me for the past twenty years you people have been hard at work shaping the present mess of world affairs?''

"You needn't sound so skeptical, Colonel. We have played no small part. Narcotics. Arms proliferation, both small and large, including nuclear. We have started wars, and ended them. The details aren't necessary. You're a smart man. Surely you know there are many things your government could never admit to knowing, much less admitting to being involved with.

"Now we, the lions, stand at the threshold of molding human history for the next thousand years. One radio call beyond the one I am prepared to make to Moscow, and we can even go nuclear. However, say we do fail at the Kremlin, even reduce Moscow to the smoldering rubble of 1942 Stalingrad. And it's fifty-fifty we may not succeed in light of the fact our army of shock troops has been sorely depleted in numbers. But we can regroup, relocate. There are other targeted countries, other targeted factions already taking our money who can be trained and armed by us and set loose on whoever or whatever we say. We fail tomorrow, well, we simply try again in the future.

"I don't have the time to discuss the finer points of our New World Order philosophy, nor debate the merits of our aims. From the monitors, I can see your strike force, and I'm assuming you and they work for my former Agency. Well, it seems you left the Antonovs intact. Thank you. Major Slobovka is en route now to prepare our evacuation. You will either be coming with us as a hostage, or as a convert. Your answer, Colonel."

Bolan held his ground in hard silence, making them wonder what he would say. It turned out the soldier would never get the chance to tell them they could go to hell.

Hell on earth delivered a sudden and unexpected opportunity for the Executioner to strike.

One, then two cameras blinked off above the Council. An air of panic seemed to paralyze the eleven would-be kings. Someone was shooting up the cameras, moving on the chamber. The muffled roar of a grenade sounded in the next moment, blowing the door apart in flying metal strips, the blast kicking the Spetsnaz commandos off their feet. An AK-47 slid up beside Bolan, who snatched it up, cocked the bolt and thumbed the selector switch for full auto. From the corner of his eye, the soldier glimpsed Ulyatin bursting through the smoke and cordite, her M-16 flaming, pinning the commandos to the floor beneath flying blood and shredded cloth.

Whirling, the Executioner went to gruesome work to delionize these predators. Their shock and fear presented him with the critical edge to annihilate the eleven in a clean sweep. Some were standing, a few were scrambling and a couple of shadows managed to draw pistols. Holding down the AK-47's trigger, Bolan swept a roaring line of 7.62 mm death over this shooting gallery of cannibals. Flank to flank, the soldier mowed them down. They toppled, sailed and screamed. Stray rounds shattered a few lights behind the dying. Sparks jumped and smoke boiled over the Council. Blood took to the air. Bodies rolled over the table, crunched up in front of Bolan.

Then Bolan caught the scrabbling sounds behind the table. His work wasn't finished. And like the man had said—it wasn't important who they were. No, it was *what* they were.

Bolan quickly picked up another AK-47 and leaped up on the platform. Ulyatin had vanished from sight, and he put her out of mind. He rolled from side to side, around the table. He found a few clawing for weapons and crushed the life out of them with lightning autofire.

The Executioner heard the fading rap of hard-soled shoes and took a quick body count. Ten. Behind the platform, a short flight of steps led to a doorway.

The soldier had the hyena on the run.

Only thing left to do was to break its neck.

McNEARY LIMPED across the body-littered, flaming ruins of the no-man's-land. Following his rooftop flight, he had landed in a slaughterbed. He had come up, firing alongside his men, at point-blank range at least a dozen Spetsnaz goons. He'd lost two more men, and Ulyatin was nowhere to be found. That firefight now seemed like an eternity ago.

What was left of Spetsnaz and Hammer's people were locked in a free-fire zone near the airfield. He left them to it. McNeary was going into the main complex to retrieve Pollock. The colonel was his kind of people.

His body on fire, bleeding like a stuck pig, having lost count of how many slugs he'd taken, McNeary trudged for the rubble of the main complex. With a fresh clip in his M-16, flanked by his men, he was hauling himself up and over the debris when the shadows boiled up out of nowhere. Firelight washing over the shadow faces, McNeary locked an angry stare with Langston. It was a frozen moment in time where all the ugly memories, all the treachery he knew this man was capable of, flamed hatred through his heart.

At the same instant Langston was raising his AK-47, McNeary and his survivors cut loose with their M-16s. The eye-to-eye firefight was deafening in his ears, and McNeary felt himself taking more lead, knew he was dead on his feet. In his dying moment, he took to his grave the satisfaction of seeing his line of slugs erupt crimson gore across Langston's chest.

BOLAN, SWIFT AND SILENT, closed on the light spilling from the doorway at the end of the short narrow hall. From beyond the door, he made out the rustling noise. One man. The sound of desperation.

He went through the door, low and firing the AK-47. The target was stuffing a satchel with black boxes, the hand holding the bag also clasping a Makarov pistol. Bolan never gave the guy the chance to fire off the first round, stitching a line of 7.62 mm doom, from crotch to sternum, on the move, closing on the dead man.

As his target slammed to the wall, crumpled to the floor, his ice blue eyes glazed with death but stayed locked in a look of feral hate. He had a shock of white hair and was somewhere in his fifties. Beyond that, Bolan didn't have a clue who he was. But he assumed he'd just taken down the voice from the light with the twisted vision of a New World Order.

The warrior found he was in a large room, but one that was tightly packed with computer terminals, radio consoles and grid maps of Russia, India and other surrounding countries—an intelligence-gathering room, no doubt. A moment later, he had to believe he'd struck the mother lode when he looked into the satchel. It was bulging with black boxes containing floppy disks. The soldier was certain that the disks contained everything Brognola would need to know about the Council, its conspiracy and whatever conspirators were out there in waiting.

Quickly Bolan retraced his steps. Back through the abattoir of the chamber, he helped himself to a half-dozen spare clips for the AK-47. He left the room, moving out into the hall beyond. Ulyatin, he thought.

The airfield. She was most likely en route to finish her vendetta with Slobovka.

It didn't escape Bolan that Ulyatin had risked her life to find him, help him turn the tide when it looked as if the noose was tightening around his neck. And if her intent had been to hunt him down and kill him, she'd had the opportunity. It stood to reason the soldier could most probably trust Ulyatin from there on.

First to find her.

He followed the distant sounds of autofire, up the long stairs, into the hall of the main complex. Alert for any sudden movement, he worked his way north. From that direction, the chatter of autofire grew, concentrated but sporadic.

Along the way, the Executioner found dead men sprawled all over the place. He made his way west, toward a smoking hill of rubble and more corpses, figuring he could use the debris for cover until he could assess the situation on the airfield.

There, he found Shiva, his men and Langston, all dead, shot up almost beyond recognition.

Venturing beyond the rubble, Bolan found the compound choked with bodies, wreckage, drifting smoke and crackling flames. Nothing moved.

Except to the north.

There, the soldier found six Spetsnaz commandos, blazing away with AK-47s. Concealed behind an armored vehicle near the tarmac, the Russians were firing at Hammer's people, who were also covered behind another AFV.

Then a third fighting party emerged from the northeast. In the firelight, Bolan recognized Slobovka. The GRU major and four other Spetsnaz commandos opened up on Hammer's people from their blindside. What was left of Bolan's friendlies never knew what hit them.

Neither did the Spetsnaz hardforce behind the AFV.

Rolling up on their rear, Bolan unleashed a raking AK-47 stream of lead hornets. Even before his last Spetsnaz victim crumpled, the soldier was sprinting for the airfield. Advancing, he glimpsed the warhead, a streaking blur coming from the northwest an instant before the missile slammed to earth near the retreating Spetsnaz. The explosive impact hit the enemy's rear, seemed to be a precision strike aimed at knocking them down.

Bolan suspected there was a good reason why the enemy hadn't been marked for easy extermination. A moment later, he found her, carried on long, angry strides for the downed enemy. Cracking a fresh clip into her M-16, Ulyatin shot Bolan a cold eye, then rolled on for eye-to-eye mop-up. The Executioner decided to let the woman take her pound of flesh.

Checking the hellzone in all directions, Bolan closed on what was left of the enemy. Under the intense firelight from the burning gunships and armored vehicles, the soldier could clearly see the pain, anger and fear on the faces of the enemy. Two of the Spetsnaz commandos lay utterly still, their eyes wide in the final call to oblivion. Slobovka was crawling along, determined to snatch up a discarded AK-47. When Ulyatin barked the GRU major's name, Slobovka snarled a curse, grabbed the assault rifle and attempted to stand. Never breaking stride, Ulyatin marched on, unleashing her M-16. She drove Slobovka to the ground, didn't stop firing until she emptied the clip.

Slowly Bolan walked up on the woman.

It seemed to take several long moments before she noticed Bolan was beside her. "Thank you, Colonel, for not interfering."

"We're even."

A moment later, Bolan found Ulyatin staring past his shoulder. Turning, Bolan found four commandos in black parkas walking toward them. Hammer's survivors but no Hammer. One of the commandos informed Bolan there was no sign of any life inside the complex. He was about to ask if any of them could fly the Antonov when Ulyatin informed him she knew how to fly the transport ship.

She glanced at the satchel around Bolan's shoulder. "I think it would be a more prudent course of action to go to Moscow rather than to return to India. If there is information in that bag about this conspiracy, then do you agree we should share it? Will you trust me?"

"I've gone this far with you—I don't see any reason to shake up the program now. Yeah, I'm with you, Agent Ulyatin."

An explosion rocked the compound. West, Bolan saw a giant ball of fire take to the sky. With the death knell of the New World Order lighting the slaughter ground, Bolan moved to board the Antonov.

The warrior couldn't be certain what awaited him on the other end. The only thing Bolan could be sure

of was that the New World Order was out of action.
For the time being.

Who knew what tomorrow would bring.

Stony Man turns the tide of aggression against
the world's most efficient crime machines

STONY MAN™ 32

LAW OF
LAST RESORT

The playground of the Caribbean becomes a drug clearing
house for an ex-KGB major and his well-oiled machine
handling cocaine and heroin from the cartels and the
Yakuza. But turquoise waters turn bloodred as Mack Bolan,
Able Team and Phoenix Force deliver a hellfire sweep that
pulls the CIA, international mafiosi and Colombians together
in an explosive showdown.

Available in January 1998 at your favorite retail outlet.

Taking Fiction to Another Dimension!

Deathlands

#62535	BITTER FRUIT	$5.50 U.S.	☐
		$6.50 CAN.	☐
#62536	SKYDARK	$5.50 U.S.	☐
		$6.50 CAN.	☐
#62537	DEMONS OF EDEN	$5.50 U.S.	☐
		$6.50 CAN.	☐

The Destroyer

#63220	SCORCHED EARTH	$5.50 U.S.	☐
		$6.50 CAN.	☐
#63221	WHITE WATER	$5.50 U.S.	☐
		$6.50 CAN.	☐
#63222	FEAST OR FAMINE	$5.50 U.S.	☐
		$6.50 CAN.	☐

Outlanders

| #63814 | EXILE TO HELL | $5.50 U.S. | ☐ |
| | | $6.50 CAN. | ☐ |

(limited quantities available on certain titles)

TOTAL AMOUNT	$
POSTAGE & HANDLING	$
($1.00 for one book, 50¢ for each additional)	
APPLICABLE TAXES*	$ _____
TOTAL PAYABLE	$ _____
(check or money order—please do not send cash)	

To order, complete this form and send it, along with a check or money order for the total above, payable to Gold Eagle Books, to: **In the U.S.:** 3010 Walden Avenue, P.O. Box 9077, Buffalo, NY 14269-9077; **In Canada:** P.O. Box 636, Fort Erie, Ontario, L2A 5X3.

Name: _____

Address: _____ City: _____

State/Prov.: _____ Zip/Postal Code: _____

*New York residents remit applicable sales taxes.
Canadian residents remit applicable GST and provincial taxes.

GOLD
EAGLE ®

GEBACK20A

Don't miss out on the action in these titles featuring THE EXECUTIONER®, STONY MAN™ and SUPERBOLAN®!

James Axler

OUTLANDERS™

SAVAGE SUN

A reference to ancient mysterious powers
sends Kane, Brigid Baptiste and Grant to
the wild hinterlands of Ireland, whose stone
ruins may function as a gateway for the alien
Archons.

But the Emerald Isle's blend of ancient magic
and advanced technology, as wielded by a
powerful woman, brings them to the very brink
of oblivion.

Available December 1997,
wherever Gold Eagle books are sold.

A deadly kind of immortality...

THE Destroyer™

#110 Never Say Die

Created by
WARREN MURPHY
and RICHARD SAPIR

Forensic evidence in a number of assassinations reveals a curious link between the killers: identical fingerprints and genetic code. The bizarre problem is turned over to Remo and Chiun, who follow the trail back to a literal dead end—the grave of an executed killer.

Look for it in January wherever Gold Eagle books are sold.